Trained together at the Athena Academy, these
six women vowed to help each other when in
need. Now one of their own has been murdered,
and it is up to them to find the killer,
before they become the next victims....

Alex Forsythe:
This forensic scientist can uncover clues others fail to see.
PROOF by Justine Davis—July 2004

Darcy Allen Steele:
A master of disguise, Darcy can sneak into
any crime scene.
ALIAS by Amy J. Fetzer—August 2004

Tory Patton:
Used to uncovering scandals, this investigative reporter
will get to the bottom of any story—especially murder.
EXPOSED by Katherine Garbera—September 2004

Samantha St. John:
Though she's the youngest, this lightning-fast secret agent
can take down men twice her size.
DOUBLE-CROSS by Meredith Fletcher—October 2004

Josie Lockworth:
A little danger won't stop this daredevil air force pilot
from uncovering the truth.
PURSUED by Catherine Mann—November 2004

Kayla Ryan:
This police lieutenant won't rest until the real killer is
brought to justice, even if it makes her the next target!
JUSTICE by Debra Webb—December 2004

ATHENA FORCE:
They were the best, the brightest, the strongest—
women who shared a bond like no other....

Dear Reader,

Enter the high-stakes world of Silhouette Bombshell, where the heroine takes charge and never gives up—whether she's standing up for herself, saving her friends from grave danger or daring to go where no woman has gone before. A Silhouette Bombshell heroine has smarts, persistence and an indomitable spirit, qualities that will get her in and out of trouble in an exciting adventure that will also bring her a man worth having...if she wants him!

Meet Angel Baker, public avenger, twenty-second-century woman and the heroine of *USA TODAY* bestselling author Julie Beard's story, *Kiss of the Blue Dragon*. Angel's job gets personal when her mother is kidnapped, and the search leads Angel into Chicago's criminal underworld, where she crosses paths with one very stubborn detective!

Join the highly trained women of ATHENA FORCE on the hunt for a killer, with *Alias*, by Amy J. Fetzer, the latest in this exhilarating twelve-book continuity series. She's lived a lie for four years to protect her son—but her friend's death brings Darcy Steele out of hiding to find out whom she can trust....

Explore a richly fantastic world in Evelyn Vaughn's *A.K.A. Goddess*, the story of a woman whose special calling pits her against a powerful group of men and their leader, her former lover.

And finally, nights are hot in *Urban Legend* by Erica Orloff. A mysterious nightclub owner stalks her lover's killers while avoiding the sharp eyes of a rugged cop, lest he learn her own dark secret— she's a vampire....

It's a month to sink your teeth into! Please send your comments and suggestions to me c/o Silhouette Books, 233 Broadway, Suite 1001, New York, NY 10279.

Sincerely,

Natashya Wilson

Natashya Wilson
Associate Senior Editor, Silhouette Bombshell

Please address questions and book requests to:
Silhouette Reader Service
U.S.: 3010 Walden Ave., P.O. Box 1325, Buffalo, NY 14269
Canadian: P.O. Box 609, Fort Erie, Ont. L2A 5X3

ALIAS

AMY J. FETZER

Published by Silhouette Books
America's Publisher of Contemporary Romance

Special thanks and acknowledgment are given to
Amy J. Fetzer for her contribution
to the ATHENA FORCE series.

 SILHOUETTE BOOKS

ISBN 0-373-51320-8

ALIAS

Copyright © 2004 by Harlequin Books S.A.

www.SilhouetteBombshell.com

Printed in U.S.A.

AMY J. FETZER

The daughter, wife and mother of U.S. Marines, Amy J. Fetzer has written over twenty-seven historical, paranormal, short contemporary and romantic suspense novels and novellas, and now she takes on adventure romance for Silhouette Bombshell. From moving across the country to across the world, Amy has a storehouse of knowledge and experience to draw on for her writing. A certified diver with five years of Shorin Ryu Karate (just in case she's attacked sixty feet underwater by a flounder), Amy has rappelled down a mountain, fired weapons and loves writing "strong heroines who know what has to be done, then do it. Believe me, a Marine wife would never wait to take action."

To the *women* of the United States Marine Corps
Our often forgotten heroines,
mothers, sisters and daughters
who strap on a helmet, a nine-millimeter,
shoulder a rifle and heft a sixty-pound pack
just like their male counterparts.

For walking into danger
and being willing to die to protect and defend
the freedom of a nation.

If that's not a true heroine,
I don't know what is.

Semper Fi

Chapter 1

Eli Archer's world was about to change.

If he'd had any smarts, he'd have left for his usual Friday night out with his pals by now. Instead, he'd stuck around his house, drinking too much too early—and that turned a redneck bully into two hundred pounds of mean and nasty.

His mistake was in taking his temper out on his small, barely nineteen-year-old wife while Darcy was less than a hundred yards away.

At the first scream, Darcy's long legs ate up the

dry, flat land, each step on her toes to make as little noise as possible. She hitched over the porch railing and stopped short of rushing through the half-open back door, then flattened against the wall. The floorboards creaked but Eli couldn't hear the noise over his own shouts. Over the degrading insults he threw at his wife, Mary Jo.

Darcy reached up and gingerly unscrewed the back-porch light, throwing the area into darkness.

She'd been watching the isolated country house from the tree line since sundown. Up close, it was worse. Sacks of garbage torn open by animals were stacked against the house. The stench of rancid grease and rotten food hung in the night air, which pulsed with swarming flies.

Darcy's eyes watered. The place reeked more of hopeless neglect. Its sagging porches and roof begged to be put out of their misery with a well-placed wrecking ball. Paint barely colored the wood exterior, the stains of the rusted tin roof streaking the sides of the building like bars caging in its inhabitants.

But a shiny new pickup truck sat in the dirt driveway, a full gun rack clear in the rear window. Easy to see where Eli's priorities lay. Darcy had already unloaded the weapons and removed the firing pins. But that didn't mean Eli Archer didn't have more. Men like him always had more weapons than guts. Predictable morons. Eli drank heavily, worked little and, for recreation, tortured stray cats and spot-lighted deer. That Eli beat his wife was a character flaw that put him just below amoebas.

A real prize.

Inside the house, Eli shouted for his boots. He was leaving. Men like him always left long enough to work up some twisted reason as to why they pounded on women—she had personal experience to back up that theory. Darcy prayed Eli went out the front door without hurting Mary Jo again. Confronting a drunken wife beater was not in her immediate plans, but she couldn't let him hurt the girl. If his mood was any indication, he'd kill her.

Darcy spied through the window for a sign of Mary Jo Archer. Shadows moved behind tattered curtains, and her heart pounded a little harder as the people inside drew closer to her position.

This was stupid. Normally, she snatched abused women while the men were gone. She could be shot for being this daring, but she couldn't abandon Mary Jo, either. And where the heck was Jack? He should have been here by now to back her up.

She moved to the open doorway, peering inside. Despite what the Archer place looked like on the outside, the interior was tidy and clean. But then how else would Mary Jane spend her time as a prisoner in her own home?

Darcy flinched when another door slammed somewhere inside, shaking the windows. She heard Eli's voice, harsh and deep as he hurled foul words at the woman he'd promised to love, honor and cherish.

Three days ago, Darcy had been woken by Mary Jo's call around midnight, the voice on the other end of the line sounding achingly familiar, hushed, terrified. Sobbing. The caller had heard from her only friend, Tomas, a worker at the local grocery store, that Darcy helped women like her. Darcy had driven like a madwoman to get there, to find Tomas and discreetly learn all she could about the Archer household. It paid to be aware of routine.

Eli met his pals at the Bullriders Saloon like clockwork every Friday night, leaving his wife locked inside the house like a punching bag he stored for his rage. He was so terrified of losing her that he'd installed latch locks better suited for a storage shed.

Pig.

That pissed Darcy off more because she understood exactly what Mary Jo was feeling right now. Terror, hopelessness. A loneliness that imbedded itself deep into her bones. And the constant worry over which insignificant detail would provoke another battle for your life.

It ends tonight.

The sound of flesh hitting flesh then a cry of pain came through the open windows and doors. Without a choice, Darcy took a breath, then stepped through the back doorway, into the kitchen. No one noticed.

Mary Jo was on the floor, scooting back out of her husband's reach, but Eli kept coming, a growling bear intent on his kill. Man, he was a big one.

Darcy slipped her knife out if its sheath. "Touch her again, Eli, and you're a dead man."

Eli whipped around, scowling mad. "Who the hell are you? Get the fuck outta my house!"

Darcy stood on the threshold. "Leave her alone."

He latched on to Mary Jo, holding her off the floor like a limp rag doll. "She's my wife, I can do what I want with her."

"No, you can't, actually. Legally or morally."

Darcy inched closer, gripping the knife, point down to slice faster and with greater accuracy. Eli didn't look the least bit intimidated by the nine-inch blade. Guns were his deal. Darcy didn't like guns. They were noisy and registered. And though she didn't really want to stab Eli, he wasn't looking very cooperative right now.

Dangling in Eli's grasp, Mary Jo whimpered, her lip bleeding.

Darcy couldn't spare a look at the woman. She kept her gaze on the man threatening them both as she moved the blade slowly back and forth, waiting for the knife to catch Eli's attention. When it did, he let his wife go, grinning as he headed toward her.

He charged like an angry bull going after the red cloak. Darcy stood her ground till he was three feet away, then sidestepped out of his path. He plowed past her into the kitchen table and landed hard on it, shattering the table legs and crashing to the floor.

Darcy rushed to Mary Jo. Keeping one eye on Eli, she grabbed the bruised, bloodied woman and tugged her to her feet, then pushed her toward the back door. "Get out of here."

"He'll kill you!"

"I'm right behind you. Go!" Darcy put herself between Eli and Mary Jo.

Mary Jo was nearly at the door when Eli rolled over, shaking his head and getting to his feet. "You bitch!"

Oh, no. For a big man, he was fast. Darcy sidestepped again, circling, forcing his attention off his wife stumbling toward the back door. Darcy'd run out the front if she had to and circle back.

Eli charged again, this time with a table leg in his hand. He swung. Darcy ducked. The table leg sang past her head, the impact driving it into the plaster wall. Eli tried jerking it out and with her elbow, Darcy clipped him in the kidney. He howled, arching with the pain, then sank to his knees. She backed toward the door, but not fast enough. He grabbed her ankle and yanked.

She hit the floor so hard her teeth clicked. The knife flew from her grip and spun across the floor.

Oh God.

"Run, Mary Jo!"

But Mary Jo, a slim blonde dressed in shorts and a T-shirt meant for a twelve year old, huddled on the edge of the room, too scared to move.

"Yeah, run, Mary Jo," Eli taunted, "so I can hunt you, too." He lunged at Darcy.

As he came down, she drove the heel of her hand up into his nose.

Cartilage shifted, bone cracked. Blood poured.

Eli Archer lurched back on his haunches, swearing and clutching his bleeding nose. "I'm gonna kill you!" he shouted, swiping his sleeve under his nose, smearing blood before grabbing for her.

But Darcy rolled away, springing to her feet, glancing around for her knife. She spotted it, but he was there, lumbering, big and hound-dog ugly.

She dove at the knife, landing on her side, grappling for it as he neared. His meaty hand latched on to her calf. He dragged her.

Darcy kicked out, struggling to reach her knife.

Eli pulled her closer to him. One smack from him and it was over. Her face would be hamburger and the latex mask hiding her identity shredded.

A crash sounded at the front of the house, the door banging against the wall just as her fingers skipped over a piece of wood. She grasped the splintered table leg and with every bit of strength she had, she swung it at his head and connected with a solid thunk.

He dropped like a stone. Darcy didn't move, breathing hard.

She heard the distinct click of a bullet moving into the chamber and looked up.

Jack Turner stood in the doorway to the living room, a huge .357 Magnum pointed at Eli's head.

"You're late." She tossed aside the wood, then crawled to her feet, annoyed with him, but glad he was here.

"A bounty got loose." His gaze flicked to her, switchblade sharp and angry. "Why the hell do you have backup if you don't wait for it?"

"He started early," she said as she retrieved her knife. Mary Jo was still in the corner, staring at her motionless husband. "You know, that was highly illegal—" she nodded toward the shattered front door "—unless there's a bounty on him."

"Oops. Wrong house," Jack said, deadpan, his weapon still trained on Eli. "That disguise is hideous by the way." His voice was low, for her ears only.

The short frosted wig and carefully applied latex face mask made her look homely. "Helps to ugly up a bit. People tend not to notice you."

His gaze moved over her body with an intensity that rivaled static electricity. "Yeah, sure."

"Let's get out of here. I don't want to wake the sleeping giant."

But Eli still hadn't moved.

"Oh, hell." Assault was one thing, manslaughter in self-defense was quite another. She inched close enough to gingerly check his pulse, but Jack stopped her.

"Leave him. He's breathing like an engine. He'll wake soon enough."

Darcy hurried to Mary Jo, pulling her off the floor.

"Who—who *are* you people?"

"You called me, remember? Come on."

When Mary Jo started for Eli, Darcy stood in her way. "Look at me. Look at *me!*" When Mary Jo did, she said quickly, "It's now or never, Mary Jo. You stay, he'll kill you."

Mary Jo nodded sharply, and Darcy pulled her to the door. They ran down the porch, and Darcy directed her toward the woods.

"Go, straight that way." She pointed, pushing her on. "Run, girl."

Mary Jo looked back at the house she'd shared with Eli for two years and her expression grew angry. Good, that's what Darcy needed to get her out alive.

Mary Jo took off, and Darcy backed up, sweeping branches across the ground to cover their tracks. Eli was a hunter, and word from the townsfolk was that he could track anything. His hunting dogs were feasting on some prime, sedative-laced USDA beef right now to keep them quiet. But that wouldn't last.

Jack rushed to her. "Go! Dammit! I'll do that." He took the branches. "He's waking up."

Darcy froze, met his gaze. "Already? He must have a head like a rock."

"So do you." Jack pushed her toward the tree line.

Darcy ran, snatching up her equipment pack, then ducking under low branches. Mary Jo was only a few yards ahead of her, crying, but moving. Darcy called softly and the girl froze, a ragged silhouette against scrubby trees. Darcy raced past, grabbing Mary Jo's hand, pulling her along, then pushing Mary Jo ahead of her. She still had to do some fast moving to get the girl safely away undetected. The two women ran, batting dry branches and skidding on crumbling ground. Then they were out in the open, vulnerable.

Darcy and Mary Jo headed straight to the edge of a ravine, stumbling down the dirt hillside to Darcy's Jeep. Darcy pushed Mary Jo into the passenger seat, tossed in her bag, then slid behind the wheel. The engine started up on the first try and she gunned it, racing away from the Archer place.

"Is he dead?" Mary Jo asked.

"No."

"Then he'll find me, I know it!" she cried.

Darcy smothered her impatience, understanding

coming quickly. "He won't find you, Mary Jo." Even if Eli had the balls to go to the police, with his record, they'd be slow to react to his claims. "I'm taking you someplace safe. Within twenty-four hours, someone will come to you at the safe house and document your abuse with photos and a statement."

She'd helped a hundred women in the last three years, from women who drove Mercedes to ones who'd never seen the inside of a hospital before and would be scarred for life. Each time, the situation seemed more desperate. More hopeless. Often, Darcy was their last chance. For some, the legal system had failed them, letting wife beaters out on bail to find the women and do it again—often resulting in death. Some were too scared to venture into the unknown without support. Or worse, they'd become so brainwashed by verbal abuse that they thought they needed these men to survive.

Mary Jo Archer had a right to be scared.

Darcy understood that kind of fear only too well.

It made her an expert at evasion and deception. Five years as a Hollywood special-effects makeup artist made her unrecognizable even now. Using disguises at every leg of a rescue protected the women's lives, as well as hers.

Darcy coveted her privacy like a fanatic. With good reason. She was a kidnapper. Plain and simple. She'd taken her baby son from his father and hidden

from the world. From her perspective, the end justi-
fied the means. Saving a life. In her case, it was two
lives.

But in the eyes of the law, *she* was the criminal.
It wouldn't matter that, before she'd escaped her
abusive husband, she'd gone to the police and filed
reports. Maurice's influence had a long reach. The
cops had dismissed her accusations, just as Maurice's family and their friends had. Maurice had
money, power and a stellar reputation as an executive film producer behind him, and in Beverly Hills
and Hollywood that put him above reproach. Above
the law.

Darcy had had nothing, and Maurice had made
sure she was trapped from all directions. Till she escaped with her friend Rainy Miller Carrington's
help.

Suddenly her throat tightened with unspent grief.
Rainy was dead. Killed in a car crash only weeks
ago. With Mary Jo's call coming soon after the funeral, Darcy hadn't even had a chance to mourn.

Rainy would be mad that I'm still hiding, Darcy
thought morosely. Even the Cassandras, her school-
mates from the Athena Academy for Women, didn't
know the full extent of her ugly past. Rainy had
known. And she'd told Kayla some of what Darcy
had gone through to escape. The others knew she was
no longer with her husband, and to them she was still

Darcy Allen Steele, hairdresser and owner of the Chop Shop Salon. She was ashamed to admit the full truth to them.

To the rest of the world, including Jack, she was Piper Daniels, an alias she'd been using for nearly three years.

Everything in my life is an alias.

A forgery, a mask to keep herself and her son, Charlie, safe and hidden. She did nothing that would alert her husband to her whereabouts and was certain he was still searching for her.

Maurice wasn't the kind of man who gave up control. Ever. Power and control were the root of who he was. And you didn't cross him without consequences.

She took a deep breath, searching for calm. She needed a clear mind for the next hours of the journey.

At least Mary Jo had a fresh chance.

"You'll file a report with the police," Darcy said, her eyes on the road, "and then disappear till Eli is behind bars."

"He *should* be in prison," Mary Jo muttered bitterly. "See how he likes it."

Darcy glanced her way. The girl's face was a mess.

Maurice had never struck her face—it would have been proof to the public that he abused her. No, he had more deadly ways of keeping her under control.

"Eli kept me in a prison for years," Mary Jo said, oblivious to Darcy's thoughts. "That house might as well have had bars."

The comment hit Darcy square in the chest.

A prison without walls. She was still locked in hers.

"Why don't you try to get some sleep." She spoke quickly to bury the feelings struggling to surface. "It's a couple hours till we make it to the safe house."

Mary Jo snuggled down into the seat. Darcy drove, aware of every flash of light in her rearview mirror. Every car they passed. Tonight, Mary Jo had her freedom.

After three years, Darcy didn't.

Because Maurice was out there. Waiting for her to slip up. Hunting her.

A pearl of fear slid down her throat.

She hated it. It tasted foul and pitiful.

And Darcy knew she couldn't live like this anymore.

But even after three years, she hadn't figured out a way to outsmart Maurice. Legally, he still had the power.

And she wasn't giving up her son, not even for her freedom.

Chapter 2

Nevada

Just past the state line, Darcy pulled into the Sleep Easy Motel parking lot, wishing it was her own driveway. But she was still hours away from Comanche, Nevada, and at two in the morning, she was bone tired, her eyes gritty.

She turned off the engine and leaned back into the seat. Mission accomplished. Mary Jo was at the safe house in Utah, and she'd zigzagged her way toward the motel to make sure that no one followed her. She'd removed the mask and wig somewhere in between when she'd stopped to grab a bite to eat. Her skin itched from the glue and all she wanted was a hot shower and a soft bed.

Grabbing her bags from the back seat, she climbed out, locked up, then headed toward her room. She stopped short when she saw a figure braced against the overhang support post outside, smoking a cigarette.

Jack Turner.

No man wore a black cowboy hat that easily.

Just seeing him made something under her skin shiver. But Darcy didn't want to be anywhere near Jack tonight. Hours in the car with her own unpleasant thoughts for company, she felt combustible. Rainy's death, the grief she'd shelved to help Mary Jo and leaving Charlie again when she just wanted to cuddle up with him and be safe had left her riddled with a mountain of emotions just waiting to crush her. Succumbing to them anywhere near Jack would just make a bigger mess of her life. He'd want to know too much, and right now, she felt weak enough to slip up.

"Well at least you didn't get arrested," she said.

He stared at her hard for a second, then pitched the smoke onto the pavement. "Don't do anything that stupid again," he said coldly.

She didn't need a reminder of the danger she'd put herself in. The bruise on her hip would do that. "I didn't have a choice. And I can take care of myself."

He sent her an arched look that said after the stunt she'd pulled tonight, he wasn't so sure. "Why do you keep doing this, Piper?"

Piper. God, what she wouldn't give to hear her own name. "Because no one else will help them."

"That's what the cops are for."

She scoffed. They'd been down this route before. Ever since that night nearly two years ago when he'd busted through a door to apprehend his bounty and found her helping a woman escape, he'd appointed himself her protector. She almost laughed. If he knew the truth about her, he'd be outta here. Or hauling her in to the police.

Darcy's only advantage was that Maurice had never filed kidnapping charges against her. She knew why—it would mean giving up control of his life if he was investigated.

"If that always worked, then they wouldn't be calling me, would they?" *Or you, bounty hunter.*

Jack moved away from the post, stopping inches from her. From under the dark hat, his China-blue gaze bored into her. He gently pinched her chin and turned her face to the side, looking for marks. "Did he hurt you?"

She stepped back, yet was touched by his concern. He looked as if he'd just about burn rubber to go avenge her.

"No, he never got the chance," Darcy said. "I

had the advantage of surprise and he was tanked already."

He folded his arms. The motion made him look bigger. "You should know by now that booze just makes them stronger, meaner—"

"But slow and off balance," she cut in. "Besides, you know that most of the time when I rescue a woman, the man isn't home."

Jack snarled something she didn't get, then said, "Were you thinking of Charlie when you confronted that ape?"

Her gaze narrowed. "Don't lecture me, Jack. You know I was. Charlie's all I have. And if you don't like the way I do things, then why are you always shadowing me?"

She didn't expect an answer. She'd asked once. He never explained and wasn't open to prying. Neither was she, so she dropped it. Though she'd tried skirting around him, he always found a way to be near. It was simply less aggravating to include him in her plans, and she admitted she felt safer with Jack and his big gun close by.

"Charlie needs his mother alive, not in a damn grave!"

His sharp tone stung, felt chastising, and she stiffened. "You think? Jeez, Jack, you act like I wanted to face down Eli. I waited as long as I could! He was going to kill her."

"And then you."

"Then be on time!"

His head snapped back, his expression taut.

She arched a brow. The air between them felt charged. Darcy felt so brittle and angry, she was spoiling for a fight.

"I'm capable of defending myself and you know it."

What he didn't know was that she'd graduated from the Athena Academy for the Advancement of Women, a private high school in Arizona that recruited exceptional girls and trained them mentally and physically to become anything they could imagine. Many Athena graduates went on to do government work, or joined the military. Darcy knew more about survival, self-defense and investigating than the average woman. While she'd never thought of herself as exceptional, she had good reflexes, strength and a sharp mind. Of the rest of the Cassandra team, two worked for intelligence agencies, one had joined the police force, one had become a national newscaster who had been recruited for government operations on the side, and one was rising fast in the ranks of the U.S. Air Force. What Darcy did for abused women was dangerous enough, but her skills were in deception. By altering her face and hair and using her acting talent from UCLA Drama, Darcy could deceive her own mother. She'd never regretted not going into the CIA when they'd come to recruit her. She had Charlie because of that choice, and though the rest of her life wasn't perfect, she wouldn't trade being his mom for any of it.

Maurice was her only regret now. He'd taken control after she'd married him, but then, she'd given some up for him to do that. Never again, she thought, even if it meant ignoring her attraction to Jack.

"Yeah, but fast and agile doesn't always match up against big and brutal."

"Don't I know it," she muttered. For a second the cool ice of his gaze softened.

He was powerful without saying a word. His rare smiles made her stomach pitch, and Charlie adored him. That alone warned her that Jack Turner was in her life too much already. Yet Jack was so unlike Maurice. He respected her views, cared less what people thought and dressed more for comfort than style—his black hat was shaped with wear, his brown bomber jacket a relic from the fifties. He was rarely without either. Or his gun.

Like her, he played everything close to the vest, as if testing people. He didn't play games. Didn't waste time or words. If she succumbed to even a scrap of her feelings, he would take her heart. And she'd made too many mistakes to invite more trouble.

"You're thinking too hard, I can tell," he said softly, his gaze riveted to her.

His gentle tone rippled over her skin, making it

tighten. "Yeah, I know." She shifted, hitched her bag on her shoulder, stuck her hands in her jacket pockets. "I have a lot on my mind." Before he could lend those big shoulders to lean on she said, "Go to your room, Jack. You must be tired, too. I'm fine."

He frowned, his gaze scouring her features as if he could see into her soul. It unnerved the hell out of her.

"You sure? You haven't been still for two seconds since you got out of that car."

She pushed her fingers into her short layered hair, unknowingly making herself look a little wilder. "Yeah, but it's nothing that some sleep won't cure."

He didn't look satisfied, yet he took her room key, opening the door and pushing it wide then leaning against the doorjamb.

Across the parking lot, the Sleep Easy neon sign sputtered and flashed, splashing blue light over him. He looked her over, long and slow, the single glance telling her he knew what she looked like naked. Darcy's insides clenched with bubbling need, her nerve endings raw near him, her body too aware of his. Desire spiraled and she closed her eyes, wishing him away, wishing he'd come to her.

She felt suddenly lost. Disconnected to everything.

No Rainy.

No freedom.

No solutions.

She raked her fingers through her hair again and gripped the back of her neck. Her eyes burned.

Damn, damn, *damn.*

"Piper?"

She slammed her eyes shut, craving to hear her own name. *Darcy,* she wanted to shout at him. *I'm Darcy Allen. I'm here, behind all these disguises and lies, I'm here!*

Then he was there. Up close. She didn't have to look to know. She could feel him, warm and male. And oh, he smelled good. Hunger flushed through her body, begging for a man's touch, to be a woman and not someone else's savior when she couldn't even be her own.

She opened her eyes, snared by the blue patience in his.

"I'm down there." He gestured to the long corridor of street-front rooms.

She didn't look. That made him too accessible—and tonight she was so on edge, she could feel it scraping up her spine and dancing on her last nerve.

She moved into the room, pulled the key from the lock and faced him.

He stayed where he was, a gentleman despite his jagged edges.

"Thanks for watching my back, cowboy," she said.

"Anytime." No pushing, no prying, just accepting

as he stepped back. She closed the door. He didn't leave till she locked it behind herself.

Darcy sighed, more with relief that she hadn't done something stupid than at the prospect of a hot shower and some rest.

She dropped her bags and headed straight for the bath.

For nearly a half hour, she let the hot spray of the shower beat down on her body, washing away the tension in her muscles. With her hands braced on the wall, head down, she forgot about Mary Jo, about Eli Archer, and let her mind wander.

It was a mistake.

Her thoughts went immediately back to Rainy. The last time she'd seen her. In a coffin. Knowing Rainy was gone forever. Having to face it. Her heart broke all over again, and she relented to her pain, sinking to the floor of the stall and sobbing like a baby.

She missed Rainy. She missed her Athena sisters. And she felt very alone and worn.

Rainy had been the best, leading the Cassandra squad when they were young, coaching them, pushing them to be stronger, better. Without Rainy, the chain felt broken. Darcy didn't have many people in her life, even fewer who knew who she really was, but Alex, Josie, Tory, Kayla and Samantha were the people she could count on in a crunch. They were bound together by more than an oath to each other. They were bound by the trials of Athena.

Pushing her hair off her face, she tipped her head back. Her heart felt like a wounded prisoner in her chest. Captured and hurting.

Turmoil boiled inside her and exploded.

She smacked the tile floor.

She wanted her life back, dammit! She wanted to hear her name spoken aloud, to stop being suspicious of everyone new in her life and constantly looking over her shoulder. She wanted to tell the Cassandras the whole truth about her marriage and wash away the shame of her weakness. She deserved better.

Charlie deserved better. Yet her own fear of losing her son kept her from finding a way to take her life back with both hands. It was by skill, caution and a hell of a lot of luck that Maurice hadn't found her yet. There was no telling what he'd do if he did. He had it in him to kill her. She'd seen that when he put a knife to her pregnant belly and threatened to kill his own child if she didn't behave. For the sake of her unborn child, she'd backed down then, smothering the urge to hit her husband.

Charlie was nearly four now, a happy, lively little boy and her entire world. He was the reason she'd planned her escape from Maurice's estate. Charlie was the reason she had bitten back her pride and called Rainy for help.

Her throat tightened, knotting like old rope.

I can't live like this anymore. With this crippling
fear. Because without her freedom, she was just a
shadow hiding in Piper Daniel's clothes.

Maurice Steele strolled through his home,
inspecting the staff's work, then setting the alarms
for the night. He was reluctant to go to bed just yet,
with the house feeling extraordinarily empty. He
supposed he should have gotten used to it, and a
starlet in his bed would have eased his solitude, but
he wasn't in the mood. Besides, he didn't want to
look at some well-used wanna-be in the morning.

He tightened the sash of his silk robe, walking
into his library, then to his desk. He collected his
papers, sliding them into his briefcase and setting
it precisely to the right of his desk before pouring
himself a brandy. He lit the warmer and set the
snifter in the holder on its side, counting off the
seconds toward perfection. The TV droned in the
background.

He lowered himself onto the sofa, propping his
feet on the table, and supposed that he was anxious
for the reviews of his latest production. He'd have to
wait. He had a fortune riding on it, and though he was
certain it was spectacular, critics had their heads up
their asses most of the time and rarely understood the
entertainment potential of an action-spy thriller.

He sipped, holding the brown liquor in his mouth for a moment before swallowing. He rarely drank more than one and never drank in public. Some people speculated that he was a recovering alcoholic because no one saw him drink liquor. Maurice never responded to the gossip. It was his personal feeling that too much explanation gave them more to speculate about, and too much drink took away the edge on the brain, the command he had of deals and productions, on or off the set.

He was leaning forward for the TV remote to turn off the set when the news anchor, relaying the recap of lead stories for the past few weeks, said one word that made his attention snap to the screen.

Athena.

He turned up the volume and listened.

Attorney Lorraine Miller Carrington was dead, a car crash. Police didn't suspect the death of the Harvard alumni attorney was more than an accident, yet gave no significant details. Maurice's eyes narrowed when they flashed a picture of "Rainy," as his wife used to call her. A pretty thing. The last time Maurice had seen her was at his wedding. They showed pictures of her in life, then one in death.

A film clip of the funeral appeared, but he didn't hear the commentary. He only saw a group of women standing outside the church. His attention focused on one, a little boy clasped in her arms. He watched, his heartbeat gaining speed. She didn't turn toward the camera, in fact, as soon as she spotted the camera she avoided it and left immediately. But Maurice had already recognized the woman's delicate profile. Her stance.

Darcy.

Well, well. The little rebel has surfaced.

He hadn't had time to study the child and he watched the clip roll to its end, hoping for another glimpse. He switched channels and after a few moments, it appeared again on another late-night station, the kind that had nothing to report but other stations' news.

Maurice leaned back, tossing the remote on the table. So. Darcy had been in Phoenix two weeks ago. With his son. Maurice had sent a half dozen private investigators after her, giving them the story that he didn't want the press to know. That she'd left in the night, with his son. But the press had found out. So had his friends, and he was left with the humiliating task of explaining away his very pretty wife's disappearance. He'd complained to his friends that he'd given her everything he had and it wasn't enough. And yes, he wanted her back. They believed him, thankfully, and he still wore his wedding ring to keep up the pretense. Maurice never hurt for feminine company—women found affairs with married men enticing—but seeing Darcy on the TV, he suddenly wanted her back under his control. Desperately.

She was too much of a rebel under all that beauty. He blamed Athena Academy and those Cassandras for that. He should never have married her, but she was poor and struggling and so lovely. He'd seen her as an uncut diamond, just waiting to be shaped and molded. He'd had to compete with a couple of men for her attention, but money made it easy. He'd seen her clothed by the finest designers, her hair styled by Hollywood's star makers. For a time, she was the perfect wife, a beautiful, sexy bride to show off.

In the back of his brain the reminder that he'd been cruel to her—that he'd shoved her down the stairs and threatened her—tried to push to the surface. But it was overshadowed by the sight of the woman who'd dared defy him. Who'd run off with his son.

She was nothing but white trash, he thought with a flash of sudden sharp anger. With a drunk for a mother and no father she could claim. And look at her—that long black dress and dark wig. Haggard, skinny. Frail. Yes, yes, it had to be her. Clearly she couldn't function well without him. He smiled slowly, pleased, knowing there was a lush, shapely body under that shapeless dress, plump round breasts on a petite frame. Dove-blue eyes in a delicate face. His little elfin princess, he thought, and for a moment he remembered having her beneath him, making love to her, nurturing her into a butterfly who had made him the envy of Hollywood.

He'd made her. She owed him.

And she was going to pay.

No one left him. No one smeared his reputation.

She'd evaded him for nearly three years, but now he had a trail. Weak, but still—it was a start. He reached for the phone, dialing, knowing exactly who owed him a favor and how to use them.

Chapter 3

Megan Pinchon's front door sprang open and Darcy couldn't get out of the Jeep fast enough as her little dark-haired boy came racing across the lawn in his Scooby Doo pajamas.

"Mommy!" He leaped at her and she caught him, crushing his body to hers, and her eyes teared as he pecked her face with kisses and made her laugh. Oh, she loved him so much. She'd been gone only overnight but it seemed much too long.

"I missed you, Mommy," he said, cupping her face and squishing it.

"I missed you, too, baby. I love you."

"Me, too. We're having doughnuts!"

She pushed back the urge to say that wasn't a healthy breakfast. "I've been dreaming of having doughnuts and I'm starving."

Megan was on the doorstep, smiling, wrapping her robe a bit tighter around her thin frame.

Darcy walked with Charlie in her arms and met her gaze. "Thanks, Meg. I love you for this."

"I know you do, honey. Come on in."

"Yeah, come on, Mom, you gotta see the puppies."

Darcy looked at Megan. "Puppies?"

"They're the neighbor boys'. Six of them."

Darcy gave her a "don't even think about pawning one off on me" look as she put Charlie down. She couldn't have a pet in a beauty salon, and since Charlie was in the salon in his play area during the day, that wasn't happening. She walked a thin line with the state board of cosmetology because while her schooling and initial license were real, the license posted in the salon was a forgery for Piper Daniels.

In the kitchen, Megan pushed a mug of coffee into her hand. "Everything okay? You look—I don't know. Different."

A good cry did that sometimes, Darcy thought, but hoped it was her new determination to break free of Maurice that showed. "I got some good sleep, I guess."

Megan wasn't fooled, but didn't push it. "Well

relax, your first appointment isn't till ten this morning."

Darcy was watching Charlie roll around with
puppies. She turned to look at Megan. "How'd you
manage that for a Saturday morning?"

Megan grinned. "I have my gifts."

Darcy smiled as Meg went to dress for work, feeling fortunate just then.

Megan Pinchon was the only person she trusted
with her son. Megan had been the common-law wife
of an abusive husband and was the first woman Darcy
had helped. By accident. Megan had been trying to
climb out the bathroom window of a fast-food restaurant to get away, and Darcy had switched clothes
with her and helped her escape. She'd given her a job
as her receptionist and a place to live till she could support herself. They'd done some healing together and
Megan had been a huge help with Charlie. She was
also the only person in Comanche, Nevada, who knew
that Piper Daniels was really Darcy Allen Steele.

She'd trained Megan to defend herself and, while
Darcy was away, to defend Charlie. She didn't have
a single doubt that Meg would protect her boy with
her life, and it made leaving a lot easier.

Darcy sipped the coffee, watching Charlie and
the six puppies again. She couldn't imagine life without him, and she had to make his world safer.

Megan came back, dressed and eating another

doughnut. The woman was rail thin no matter how much she stuffed in her mouth. It was maddening.

"Ahh, now there's a grin." Meg pointed with the half-eaten doughnut. "Since Rainy's death, I didn't think I'd see that again."

Darcy turned to her, pushing her hair off her face. "Me, either." It was hard to believe the funeral had been nearly two weeks ago.

Her brows knit as she freshened her coffee, the night Rainy died rolling back.

"I'm calling on the Cassandra promise," Rainy had said on the phone. They'd made the pact as teens, that when one of them called for help they would come, no questions asked. "Meet at the Christine Evans bungalow." Christine was the principal of Athena Academy, and her bungalow was on school grounds. Darcy had bought tickets to Phoenix, Arizona, the nearest city, immediately.

Rainy had insisted on secrecy. That alone told them something was up. Alex, Kayla and Josie were there before Darcy had arrived with a sleepy Charlie. Christine hadn't known what Rainy wanted to talk to them about and only mentioned searching the school records.

Exactly why Rainy wanted to meet with them at the principal's house they never learned. She was killed in an accident just an hour before the appointed time. Darcy swallowed, holding back new tears. Car crash my fanny, she thought, growing angry again.

None of the Cassandras believed the doctor's report that Rainy had fallen asleep at the wheel and crashed.

Alex, a forensic scientist with the FBI, had observed Rainy's autopsy. Alex had discovered that the appendectomy Rainy had supposedly had during her first year at Athena had been a fake. She'd also noticed severe scarring on Rainy's ovaries.

Rainy's husband, Marshall Carrington, had revealed that he and Rainy had been trying for years to have a baby. Recently Rainy had begun fertility treatments. Her doctor had told them Rainy had scarring on her ovaries that would make it hard for her to conceive. The doctor had thought it the result of a natural physical problem. The Cassandras now suspected, as Rainy must have, that her eggs had been harvested when she was only a girl and the scarring was a result of that monstrous crime.

Automatically her gaze swung to Charlie rolling around on the grass with another little boy and six fat black puppies. She could almost feel her heart break for Rainy. Charlie was her whole world and she understood her friend's need for a baby.

But it was depraved that someone would violate a twelve-year-old girl for her eggs. And the Cassandras were certain that someone had taken the eggs for a reason. God, with the technology, it could be any number of options and experiments. The thought turned Darcy's stomach.

Rainy's doctor had also left town suddenly, and Alex and Kayla's efforts to find out her whereabouts had so far come to nothing. And what about Kayla fainting while on Athena grounds just before the funeral?

Darcy made a mental note to call Kayla sometime today to see if she'd learned something more. The one thought repeating in her mind was, if someone had fertilized Rainy's harvested eggs, in-vitro or perhaps via a surrogate, then there was a real possibility that Rainy had a child out there somewhere.

Darcy's skin chilled. If Rainy found out and had been killed to keep it quiet, then it was murder. The questions the Cassandras had to answer were who had harvested the eggs and why.

Oh, Rainy, she mourned, covering her mouth and fighting fresh tears. *You knew, didn't you?*

Before you died, you knew.

Her throat tightened, and suddenly, Darcy pitched her coffee and stepped off the back porch. Kicking off her shoes, she called to Charlie and plopped down in the grass. The puppies hopped all over her and she lay flat, letting them lick their fill.

But it was Charlie's sweet giggles that melted the pain in her heart.

* * *

The Chop Shop was humming, with four stylists hard at work and more clients waiting to be pampered. The atmosphere in the fifties garage-style salon, complete with cheesecake posters and retro fittings, invited fun and drew a wide variety of clients.

The doors on the stylists' work stations were old car doors, cut to fit, the handles authentic. The chairs were comfy car seats upholstered in electric blue. Even her appointment desk was the chopped-off front end of a Cadillac, complete with windshield. The walls were high gloss with four-foot-wide tear stripes in hot pink, electric blue and neon green between wide paths of black, toned down by the black-and-white checkerboard floor. Neon signs with the shop's name hung outside and in the front window.

Darcy had put her mark on everything, from the black work aprons with the shop's name emblazoned in hot pink to the play area for Charlie and her customers' kids. Yet she longed for the day when she could add her real name to the proprietress sign tacked near the front door.

She passed the picture of the previous owner, Crystal Hart, smiling, knowing Crystal would approve of the new look and name. Darcy loved the salon because Crystal had taken her in, given her a job and kept her secrets. The older woman had been more interested in helping her with Charlie than doing hair and to Charlie, she'd been more of a grandmother than Darcy's own mother. Which wasn't hard, she thought, sectioning off a client's wet hair for a cut. Delores Allen had her nose deep in a fifth of scotch by noon every day. Darcy shook off thoughts of her mother and started cutting.

For less than two short years, Darcy had been graced with Crystal's wisdom and kindness. Then Crystal had been diagnosed with cancer. When her health declined, Darcy took over the business for her. Crystal's dying wish had been for Darcy and Charlie never to have to hide behind an alias again.

Darcy was determined to get her life out of this holding pattern.

Around her, blow-dryers whined and the strong scents of tint and bleach permeated the air. Fifties music played in the shampoo area in the back of the salon while the television entertained the clients in the front.

She trimmed her client's hair, not paying attention to anything but the cut. Charlie was corralled in his play area with another customer's child, coloring.

Her client spoke up. "Oh, there's that thriller movie that's coming out. I want to see it. Ben Collier is to-die-for cute."

Darcy barely glanced up at the TV as the entertainment segment came on. She kept trimming hair.

When she glanced up again, she saw the Steele Productions Presents logo and her heart slammed in her
chest.

Maurice.

There was a brief theatrical trailer for the action-
spy thriller before the commentator said, "Critics
are calling the high-budget film *Dead Game* the action thriller of the year. Ben Collier delivers a surprisingly stellar performance that some say will
make him the next box-office king. The film com-
bines a tremendous script, daredevil action and
breathtaking locations. The film world is breath-
lessly awaiting this release because recent Pegasus-
backed films involving Ben Collier and executive
producer Maurice Steele haven't had the expected
box-office draw in recent years. Sources tell us that
Steele cofinanced this film himself with financier
Porche Fairchild."

Darcy went still, listening. In the past, Maurice
had used his business assets and connections to back
a film that studios didn't want. Most often they came
crawling back to him when the film was nominated
for Oscars. She had to give him credit, he could spot
true talent. He liked to have enough money invested
that he had control of the film, too.

But it wasn't until the reporter again mentioned
production financier Porche Fairchild that Darcy excused herself from her client and moved closer.

She turned up the volume.

"Ms. Fairchild has been on sabbatical in Europe, and while her sudden disappearance was at first suspicious, authorities say the doubt has been clarified. Yet, since October three years ago, the reclusive Ms. Fairchild has yet to come forward and show herself."

A picture of Porche Fairchild flashed on the screen. Small, blond and sophisticated. And missing?

"In the financial world, Miss Fairchild was known for bankrolling large-scale productions, but her decision to finance this film with Steele Productions, whose last few films had flopped, became gossip for the rumor mills." Darcy saw pictures of Maurice and Porche Fairchild shaking hands. Three years out of sight? Didn't anyone miss this woman? The police must have investigated, Darcy thought, and proven her existence.

"Maurice Steele had no comment other than how delighted he was to work with Porche and would love to again, and that he hoped she'd make the premiere. The good news for Ben Collier is the prerelease reviews are tremendous. The widely publicized premiere is scheduled for later this month and *Nightly Entertainment* will be there to show you all the glitz and glamour of the event."

"Piper? You okay?"

Darcy nearly dropped her scissors as a niggling

memory flashed in her mind. She looked around. Customers and stylists were staring at her. She flashed a brittle smile and excused herself, hurrying to the back supply room.

Megan stepped in after her, closing the door.

"My God, Darcy, you're pale."

She waved that away. "Do you remember those plastic bags of stuff in your deep freeze?"

"Yeah, they're still there. It's clothes and papers, isn't it?" Megan put her hands on her hips. "I never understood why you kept that stuff."

"Because they're Maurice's clothes, his papers and a computer disk of pictures from when he beat me. It's evidence I thought I could use someday. After all this time, I just forgot it was there."

"So what's got you so jittery?"

Darcy peeked out and told her client she'd be right there, then moved away from the door.

"Three years ago, Maurice was out very late one night. That was nothing big, he was always wheeling and dealing with actors and directors till dawn sometimes. But this time, when he came back, he was hugging his briefcase like a lifeline. When the maid tried to take it for him, he refused."

"I'm still stunned you had a maid, you know. I've seen you scrub toilets."

Darcy smiled, realizing she'd indeed come full circle since then. "Maurice snapped at me not to disturb him, then went to his library. Then he started drinking."

"I don't see your point. From what you told me, Maurice was controlling."

"It's not the briefcase or his attitude, but the drinking was odd. Normally he'd nurse one drink all night, because he never wanted to be drunk and lose control over himself. But what I noticed was that he wasn't wearing the same clothes he'd left in that morning."

"Okay, *that* you didn't mention."

"He often went to the gym with a client after work, so I didn't think much of it until I found him passed out in the chair and the clothes in the fireplace."

"The fireplace? He burned his clothes? Was he passed out naked?"

"No, he burned the clothes that he left wearing *that* morning. They must have been in his briefcase."

"Is that what's in my freezer?"

"Yeah. And he had scratches on his hand, too."

"Could it have been a bar fight? Or something with an actor or whoever?"

Darcy roared back. "Maurice? He wouldn't dare make a public display like that. He'd rather die than lose his cool or his reputation."

Megan folded her arms and leaned back against the counter. "See, that's the difference between Saul and Maurice. Saul wouldn't have thought for a second about bashing me in a bar full of people."

Darcy touched her arm, sympathetic. "Maurice would. He rarely raised his voice. He was all about threats and locks and hitting me where no one else could see it."

"So why was he burning the clothes, do you think?"

"I don't know." Darcy paced in the small room, driving her fingers through her short, dark hair. "I wanted out, Meg, and I'd been planning it for a while." She'd stolen enough of his insomnia medication over the last months to knock him out, had stashed money and clothes and was just waiting for the moment when she could call Rainy and disappear with her baby. "When I saw the burned clothes I thought, if he's burning a two-thousand-dollar suit and a silk shirt, something must be up. So I took them. Then I copied his date book for that week and replaced the burned clothes with something similar I was giving to charity."

Darcy laughed uneasily. "I even burned them to make it look good. He woke when the maid was cleaning it up in the morning and made some excuse that I didn't hear. She dumped them in the trash."

"The maid thing is still throwing me," Megan said with a smile. "We can get the bags out tonight after closing. But what do you think you'll find?"

"I don't know. Rainy came and helped me get

away a couple days after that, so I was spending all my time with Charlie and trying to get my strength back."

"So give me your best theory."

"Porche Fairchild committed millions to a movie deal with Maurice. I heard him talking to her on the phone a few times. And she's been missing since October, three years ago."

"Missing?"

Darcy told her about the entertainment news report. "They say she's accounted for, but no one has seen her. I left Maurice in October, Meg. And Maurice made the deal with her in October and she vanished right around the same time."

"You think he killed this woman, don't you?"

"He had it in him. If I can prove Maurice had something to do with Porche's disappearance, he'll go to jail and Charlie and I will be free."

Megan wasn't convinced. "That's a really big *if,* Darcy."

"A huge one, I know. It's a lot to prove." Short of going to Europe to find the woman, which she couldn't afford to do, Darcy had to prove the connection between Maurice and Fairchild that night, and well, sadly, hunt on the premise that Fairchild was dead.

"I need to get back to work."

"Yeah, and you need to stop drinking so much caffeine, too."

Darcy laughed softly as they left the room, but she had a hard time concentrating on anything but those freezer bags of evidence to a crime Maurice *might* have committed.

That's as weak as it got, she thought, but it was a start. She had to move quickly. She couldn't say why, but she had the distinct feeling that time was about to run out.

Chapter 4

Sunday was a day of rest for most people, but Darcy was anxious to start searching.

Her fingers flew over the keyboard as she tracked Maurice's recent activities easily, bringing up pictures of him coupled with the starlets in his films. She didn't doubt for a second that he'd cheated on her back when they'd been together. He had his hands up a lot of skirts and in too many pockets. It was one of the reasons she couldn't get help. Too many people owed Maurice and he owed just as many. Asking the wrong person would have alerted Maurice to her plans.

This morning, she'd already investigated the

pages she'd copied from Maurice's date book, but there wasn't anyone listed who wasn't still alive and visible. She dug deeper, Web Detective helping her along. Flipping through the archived pictures of *Variety,* she saw one with Maurice's chauffeur in the background. He'd never gone anywhere without the driver—the man was his paid muscle, content to stand by the car and wait till needed. Darcy hadn't paid much attention to him because Maurice never allowed him to speak to her directly. She wondered how loyal he really was to Maurice and made a note to find out somehow.

She almost considered calling Jack for help, but it was still early. He'd been teaching her how to investigate so she was better prepared to rescue women and bring them safely into the underground network. First rule of investigative work, he'd taught her, was follow the money trail and document it on paper. And Maurice had a path a mile wide behind him.

She worked the Internet, looking through the new movie's Web site, the past film sites; pulling up his public financial status, she almost laughed. Maurice was rich as sin, but the report showed that he was just comfortable. Oh, yeah, pay for a four-million-dollar estate in Beverly Hills on that, and bring the IRS in full force. It proved to her that Maurice was clever, and devious. Capable of anything.

And just why did I marry this man? The same answer came. He was handsome, rich, a powerful movie producer, and while he could have had any woman, he'd chosen *her*.

He'd had his reasons, though she hadn't seen it then. He thought he could mold and control her and, in a way, he had. He'd given polish and sophistication to a girl whose father was just a scribbled name on a birth certificate and whose mother was a drunk. Since Maurice still kept her mother loaded and in luxury, Darcy didn't consider calling her. She'd tell Maurice just to keep those cushy surroundings.

And why not?

Life on Maurice's estate was a far cry from Darcy's youth of living in cheap apartments and being evicted when her mother lost jobs because of her drinking. Delores had constantly mourned the loss of her beauty, spending more time with "I remember when" than working to improve herself or at least get into a rehab center. Delores had been married three times and thought she needed a man to be whole. Darcy knew otherwise. Sometimes, when it was really bad, she'd lashed out at Darcy, blaming her birth for all her troubles. It was painful to hear, and the booze was doing the talking, she knew. But for a long time, she'd believed it.

She pushed herself to make good grades, as if that would win her mother's love and make her stop drinking. Of course, it hadn't. When she was invited to attend Athena Academy, all expenses paid by the school, she'd thought she'd been granted asylum in a foreign country. Athena made her see her own potential. Maurice had slowly taken that away.

God I was a sap, she thought, disgusted, and she focused on finding information on Fairchild.

An hour later she learned something surprising.

Porche Fairchild was not who she seemed. Though the name said money and affluence, Porche's real name was Patty Fogerty. She'd changed it legally just before receiving her MBA and stepping into the business world. Like Darcy, she'd gone to college on scholarships and had worked a job, as well, interning with William Morris Agency. From the records of investments, Porche had done some creative financing, and while Darcy couldn't see anything wrong in the numbers, it made her wonder how she'd become so rich so fast and why she'd then vanished. Was she into something illegal, something that had forced her to skip out before she was caught?

There wasn't a single article or mention of Porche in any magazine or newspaper in three years, and the two she did find were about her sudden absence from the financial world. An undisclosed spokesman's statement said that Ms. Fairchild was on sabbatical.

Bunk. It was sad that the absence of a bright

young woman with a great mind would go unnoticed for so long. Porche didn't have any family. Darcy wondered if there'd been anyone she could depend on, someone who might have cared enough to file a missing person's report.

The image hit a little close and Darcy grew more determined to find out what happened to the woman.

The only other mention was an old piece in *Variety* and a production notice. So if Fairchild's finance business was closed, what had happened to her accounts, her money? Her home? Checking her last known address brought up a real-estate listing. The house had been sold three years ago and was up for sale again.

Nice digs, Darcy thought, noting the Bel Air address. She called the real-estate agent but the woman wasn't forthcoming on the circumstances, which raised her suspicions. Darcy made another call to Porche's former office number and got a deli somewhere in Fremont, CA. She found an old staff listing and called Fairchild's assistant, Marianna Vasquez, but the woman worked for a bank and was away on business. She made a note to call her later.

She struck gold when she surfed free credit reports and learned Porche's last open personal transaction was two nights before Maurice had come home hugging his briefcase.

While film and movie finances weren't public

record, Darcy went out on a limb and tried to access the personal accounts she'd shared with Maurice.

Maurice had changed the pass code, but after a few tries, she found that it was only by two digits. Idiot. She hit the key and the screen blinked to life. Pages and pages of account history scrolled past.

"Well, well, look at that money trail, Maury."

Darcy smiled, typing in the dates to narrow the field. She kept bringing the search down tighter and tighter, and her eyes blurred from reading so many numbers.

Maurice had been a wealthy man when she married him, and she'd had unlimited funds and all the perks that went with them. Now, Maurice could afford three wives and she wondered when enough was enough. Twenty million? Thirty? Of his last three movies before *Dead Game*, Maurice had coproduced only the last two. Apparently the studios had lost enough confidence that he'd had to go to Fairchild for the third, *Dead Game*. Maurice would have had to convince her to finance the film.

Darcy's eyebrows knitted and she sat back, remembering he'd been having trouble getting funds because, while the script was good, the star, Ben Collier, hadn't had much success. Thirty-five million in production was a lot to ride on maybe.

She glanced at her freezer. Megan had given the bags to her last night and Darcy was so tired and busy with Charlie that she'd just thrown them in there. She knew she needed more than burned clothes to back up her theory. She had to be extremely careful. Her life and her son's depended on it.

Darcy saved the file and printed the documents, then left her small home office to wake Charlie. She couldn't do much else from Nevada. Though she didn't want to be in the same state as Maurice, she had to do some firsthand snooping. She needed some special equipment, she thought, kissing her son awake.

And she knew just who to call.

Darcy threw open the door and smiled. Jack blinked as if stunned.

"What?"

"Been a while since I've seen you smile like that, I guess. It looks good on you."

His gaze flowed over her body. In jeans and a strapless red top, she must look pretty silly, considering it was cold outside.

"Thanks for coming, Jack." She pushed open the screen door. "Come in."

Removing his hat, he stepped inside. "You going to tell me what you need all this camera equipment for?" He offered her a black duffel bag.

"No, not really. Does it matter?" Darcy really didn't know if she was going to need it, but she wanted to be prepared.

"Just don't implicate me in anything illegal."

She rolled her eyes, taking the bag. "And here I thought you were the adventurous type." She walked down the hall to the kitchen, inclining her head for him to follow. She could feel his gaze on her, as if it were rubbing over her skin. It made her insides tighten and she busied herself with getting him some coffee.

He readily accepted, groaning as he sipped.

"Tough night gathering the bad guys?" She sipped her own.

"Paperwork." He glanced around the kitchen. "What's all this?" He motioned to the bucket on the kitchen table, then peered into it. "Plaster?"

"I'm making faces, masks." Her kitchen looked like a lab and she wondered at the wisdom of having him here right now.

"Mind if I hang around and watch?"

She hesitated for a second. "No, of course not. Actually I'd love a little help keeping an eye on Charlie since I'm alone."

"No problem. Where is he?"

"Living room. Cartoons and grape juice."

Jack set his cup down and gave her a look that said, can I see him? She smiled and nodded, following Jack into the room.

They found Charlie in his pj's, tucked in a corner of the sofa like a bunny burrowed in for the winter.

His face was smeared with jelly, a half-eaten piece of toast in his hand. Darcy didn't think Jack would get a rise out of her son, he wasn't interested in anything but the cartoons. She was wrong.

"Hey, pal."

Charlie looked up, grinning widely. "Jack!" He shot off the couch and plowed into Jack's knees.

Jack lifted him and her son looked so tiny in his arms. "So what's with this?" He pointed to his chest, and when Charlie looked down, Jack nudged his nose up.

Charlie giggled and something inside her fell a little harder for Jack. He was so good to Charlie.

"You wanna watch *Transformers* with me?"

"Maybe later, I'm going to help your mom for a bit. If that's okay."

Her son looked disappointed for a second till the cartoon came back on. Jack set him down, then followed Darcy back to the kitchen.

She added more plaster powder to the water, stirring.

"So explain this."

"I've got to make a fresh cast of my face in relief before I can build a mask. My old form is getting mushy." She gestured to the plaster head and shoulders sitting on a stand that secured it to the edge of the table.

"I make a relief of my own face, then make a cast from that and put it on the head form. It's hard and solid. Then with soft latex and foam, I build a new face on top of that. That way it fits over mine without any wrinkles or gaps."

"Can you put that stuff on anyone?" From a plastic box, he picked up a fake nose, a chin and half a lip.

"Yeah, in a crunch, but you have to fill in the space between the skin and the latex with a fast-drying foam and it leaves it hard, so the facial features don't move with the wearer. It has to be thin where it contacts with the major muscles of the face, so it moves with expressions. If it doesn't fit, it sort of defeats the purpose. Too noticeable."

He took up his coffee, his gaze moving over her equipment. "I've seen you in these masks a lot, but you never said where you learned all this."

She stopped stirring for a second, then continued. "I wanted to work on movies and took a course."

It was a bald-faced lie, Darcy thought, but she couldn't say more. Nor could she look at Jack and say it. It was hard to lie to him, even if it was to protect herself and Charlie.

"Over the years, I've just gotten better at it, studied, tried different approaches." The truth was Darcy had worked on movies for a few years before she married Maurice, then a couple after. She'd studied acting in college, and had gotten a couple of good minor roles in films, but she preferred the hair, makeup, and mostly, special-effects facial mechanics.

"Is this human hair?"

She glanced up, struggling with the mix as the plaster thickened. He held a sample from her selection of bound locks of hair. "Yeah, I have to put each hair in individually to make the hairline look authentic. Then put on a wig and blend the hair so there's no line."

Jack sipped his coffee, picking up the facial mask she'd used the other night, then riffling through the box of wigs and hairpieces. Darcy even had stuff to make her look like a man.

"You really think all this will protect you?"

"It has so far." He was more interested in watching her than the process, she thought.

"I think that roundhouse kick and your wicked knife do more."

"I do this to avoid being recognized. No one can trace me."

"Stopping altogether would help."

"You walk into danger every time you hunt a bounty, so just because I'm a woman—"

"A woman with a child to think about."

Darcy groaned, stirring. "Leave it alone, Jack."

"I just don't want to see anything happen to you, Piper."

"Why?"

He pulled out a chair and sat, sipping his coffee. "If I have to say, then you're not as smart as I thought."

She met his gaze and wondered why she always felt stripped naked when he was near. "Must you stare?"

"You're an exceptionally pretty woman, why shouldn't I stare?"

She gave him a dry look. "It's confirmed, your taste is all in your mouth. I look like a drowned rat." She fluffed her hair and Jack leaned over the table.

"Why is it so hard for you to take a compliment?"

She met his gaze head on. "I haven't had many."

His eyebrows shot up and those intense eyes roamed her body from feet to hair. "Maybe they didn't have the guts to say."

"Why would you think that?"

"It could be the barrier around you that's better than a castle wall."

She looked him over, liking what she saw too much. "A girl has to protect herself from those unseemly types."

"Ouch."

She motioned him close and he set aside the coffee and came to her. "Here's where you come in. I'd take off your jacket if I were you."

He stripped out of the bomber jacket and hung it on a peg by the back-porch door with his hat. His

T-shirt stretched tight across those massive shoulders and bulging muscles and Darcy almost lost her train of thought just looking at him.

He arched an eyebrow, the look saying he caught her staring. Hurriedly, she slipped on a headband that pulled her hair back off her face, then wrapped her hair in a turban.

"Unattractive, I know." She sat in the kitchen chair. "I'm going to apply the first layer, but when I get to the places around my nose and mouth and ears, can you do the rest?"

"Sure. Just tell me how."

She explained that there couldn't be any air pockets and to tap the plaster lightly to get them out. "And I won't be ignoring you if you talk—I can't answer, lip movement destroys the details."

She scooped up a blob of the plaster and started smearing it over her hairline, her jaw, throat and then down onto her chest.

"That far?" he said.

That was why she wore the strapless top. When she'd covered nearly all of her face, she inserted two straws into her nose so she could breathe, then motioned for him to add more. Jack rolled up his sleeves and spread plaster.

She had a notepad on her lap and a pencil to scribble advice. She felt his touch, the gentleness of it belying his big hands as he made sure the plaster was in and around her ears, and then down on her throat and lower.

Don't get fresh, she wrote when his hand smoothed over the swells of her breasts. Her nipples tightened and her mind went into fantasyland when he kept smoothing the cool plaster slowly.

"I'm just doing what you want, Piper."

Not quite, she thought, and reached to inspect the thickness and texture, making certain she was completely covered.

"How long do we wait?" he asked.

She scribbled, *Till it dries, dingy. 20 mins.* The fan set up close by hastened the process. Then she wrote again, *Eye on Charlie, likes to jump on the couch.* She heard Jack's soft chuckle and barely made out his footsteps as he walked away.

Darcy tried to relax and be still, yet her mind was running at full speed. She didn't like that she couldn't see Jack or what he was doing. But she could feel him when he came close. When the mold was done, she tapped the table and he was there to help her lift it off.

"I hate that part, makes me feel like I'm buried alive."

She stood and placed the relief in a frame padded with cotton, then excused herself to wash up and change into a T-shirt. When she came back Jack was exactly where she'd left him.

"Charlie? You want some eggs or cereal?" she said as she tipped the relief so it was level and started building barriers around it with thin sheets of metal and pins.

"Toaster tarts!" he called back and Jack chuckled.

"Oh, I so don't think so." Bending, she inserted metal frame pins to hold the irregular shape in place.

"Mom," he whined.

"Pick one, kiddo."

"Eggs," Charlie said, sulking as she started mixing chemicals and plaster.

"You look like a mad scientist with all that," Jack said.

"This will make the face form mine, in relief. It's plaster, but it has a liquid plastic hardener that will make it come out of the mold and stay hard. Then I'll just take the old head form, cut the face off, and apply a fresh one."

"Yes, Dr. Mengela."

Her chuckle was sinister as she slowly blended the plaster with a kitchen hand mixer. "Then I mix up the polymer clay and with some foam, start building the face."

"Should I be concerned that you'll develop dual personalities?" he asked, lifting a full mask of a man's face.

She smiled. "No, I like being a woman. I put that on the women I help, Jack, so the trail vanishes and nothing can be traced back to here, and Charlie."

"But this underground railroad you're part of—"

"Don't mention the illegalities, please." He harped on that a lot.

"You said it, not me. What if something happens while you're moving through it? It's so secret even the cops can't find the trail."

"Why would they want to? Safe house means in secret. A lawyer and a cop come to the women and take pictures and statements at a different location. It's a requirement to remain at the safe house that they file formal charges and appear in court if they have to."

"They'd like to have authority over it. Make sure nothing gets thrown out of court on a technicality."

"Hasn't yet."

Jack moved to the stove, pulling out a small frying pan. "Man, you are so stubborn."

"Look who's talking." Darcy looked over her shoulder, her expression questioning.

"Charlie's eggs."

"Thanks. Scrambled."

"Oh good, the only kind I can do."

"Make some for yourself if you want."

Darcy felt weird. He'd been here before, just not for long and certainly not cooking in her kitchen. She didn't want to think about how comfortable it felt to have him here. When he was done, he cleaned up and took the plate to Charlie, and since the kitchen table was occupied with her latex, he had Charles sit at the coffee table. Then he plopped down beside her son and joined him.

Darcy's heart did a little leap at the way he looked at her son. Charlie's own father hadn't even held him when he was born. Maurice demanded she abort and when she refused, he threw her down the stairs, hoping she'd lose the baby. Pushing her kept his hands clean. An accident, he'd say. The memory blasted through her and she flinched, feeling each bang of the steps. Curling her body into a ball to protect her baby, the cool tile floor beneath her cheek.

"Piper?"

She blinked. Jack was standing close, holding the empty plates. How long had she fazed out?

"You all right?"

Tears burned her eyes and she quickly looked away. "Yeah, fine. Got powder in my eyes, I think."

Jack didn't believe her, she could tell, yet he soaked a towel for her. "Let me see."

"It's fine now."

"Let me see," he insisted and tipped her face up, then blotted the wet cloth over her eyes. There was nothing there, but he pretended there was. He eased the cloth from her eyes and she opened them. Her vision filled with him.

"Okay?"

Darcy breathed him in, his strength, his scent. His face was so close, his mouth inviting. His gaze raked her face, as if searching for answers she knew he wanted. But he didn't say anything.

Then his head dipped, his mouth a breath from hers.

"Don't, Jack." Yet she didn't back away.

"Don't what?"

"Oh, I know you're not stupid and neither am I. Don't take this friendship there."

"Are we friends, Piper? I figured I was just the hired muscle."

"Yeah, that, too." She eased away from him. Instantly she felt more alone.

"Friends trust each other."

"I trust you with my life, Jack."

His look went sour. "You give that to cops and firefighters."

"What do you want from me?"

"To know you."

"You do."

"No, I don't." He gestured to the array of chemicals and powders, makeup and fake hair spread across her kitchen. "I'm wondering if anyone does."

Darcy didn't say anything. Because it was true. No one really knew who she was, least of all her. Jack stepped away, reaching for his jacket and hat. Darcy cleaned off her hands and walked him to the door.

He had his hand on the knob when he said, "By the way, I saw Charlie on TV last week."

And the bottom of her world fell out.

Chapter 5

"And you, too."

Darcy froze. "You must be mistaken."

"I know it was you, because you don't let anyone near your son except Meg. But it was Charlie I recognized."

Darcy felt instant and overpowering panic. Her knees went soft and she struggled for calm.

"That's not possible, Jack."

"It was a sound bite about a woman who was killed in a car crash. A lawyer." He frowned slightly, thinking. "She went to that women's school, the one that trains girls for spy work…Athena Academy, then Harvard."

"You couldn't have seen him."

Jack moved closer, hemming her in, his cool stare leaving no doubt of what he saw. "I did, Piper. It was Charlie, and you were at that funeral."

Cornered, she let out a long breath and muttered, "Yes, I was."

"You went to Athena Academy?"

"Me? No, no I didn't. I knew Lorraine Carrington from college."

His gaze thinned. "She went to Harvard."

"Only for law school." Another lie, she thought, a thousand problems shooting through her mind.

Jack was scowling now. "You can't even give me a straight answer, can you? Why can't you trust me?"

"I don't trust anyone," she snapped and stepped back. "And butt out of my private life, Jack. Or I'll start prying into yours and you can tell me how you got that bullet hole in your shoulder."

His expression shuttered, he moved to open the door. "Fine. But I want you to know I'm here to help you if you need it."

"With what? I don't need it."

"Yeah, sure. When you're ready to tell me why you constantly look over your shoulder, why you're terrified right now, we'll talk again."

"No, we won't."

Jack cast her a dark glance that made her shiver. Not talking wasn't up for debate in his eyes and

Darcy wondered how long she could avoid it. He left and she shut the door after him, sinking against the wall.

Oh damn. Damn.

What were the chances of anyone else recognizing her and making a connection?

Darcy headed back into the kitchen, her hands shaking. She'd covered her tracks, she knew she had.

Pay cash, use disguises, don't make conversation with strangers for long. Check everyone out. The last thought reminded her that she hadn't done that with Jack. All she knew of him was what she'd learned since the moment they'd collided on a rescue till now. And now he knew she'd been at Rainy's funeral. She hadn't worn a mask when she'd gone to Arizona, because she'd been among friends, not rescuing a woman from a dangerous attacker.

This pushed her plan to go to L.A. next week to sooner than she wanted. She had to work fast in case Maurice had seen the broadcast and found a way to track her from Arizona to here.

If he did, she was history.

One week later
Hollywood

Dressed in a berry-colored designer skirt and top she'd bought at a secondhand store on Rodeo Drive,

Darcy sat under the covered porch of a bistro, sipping her soda and watching the people stroll by.

She recognized several: a couple of agents, one action-adventure actor who shouldn't be wearing leather pants anymore. She remembered making him look as if he'd been burned for his third film. She brought the glass to her lips, liking that men were noticing her, but then she wore another's face. A little closer to Julia Roberts today.

This morning she'd been a bag lady pushing a shopping cart outside Maurice's offices. She'd gone there to watch his daily routine, and fortunately, it hadn't changed. She was almost nabbed when the cops showed up, but instead of hauling her in for vagrancy, they'd escorted her to a women's shelter. If she wasn't so terrified that Maurice would spot her, she'd be amused that she could slip around the city within thirty yards of the man. She'd no intention of getting any closer.

From her position, Maurice's chauffeur wasn't hard to spot. He wore a gray uniform while all the others lined up on the street in the hills wore black. He was the same man who'd worked for her husband when they'd married.

Oh goody. She paid her bill and stood. She'd used everything at her disposal to do what she needed, and right now she had it all displayed in a slim hip skirt with a matching top, cut low and fitted to accent her waistline. Time to put the ball into play, she thought, walking toward the limo, aware that Maurice was inside a restaurant just up the street.

A little nervous twinge swept up her spine. She was afraid that if she saw him, she'd walk up to him and punch his lights out. Instead she strolled toward the driver, hips swaying, and her long legs in spike-heel sandals drawing attention. She rarely showed her body off like this, it practically screamed available and desperate.

She stopped, waiting till the driver noticed her. When he did, her resolve slipped a little.

It's a role, she thought, and everything had to have a purpose. Coyly, she chewed her lip, glancing left and right, then sauntered up to him.

"Hi, there." A French accent did nicely this time.

"Hey yourself." He squinted through the smoke from his cigarette, then straightened, obviously thinking she was *that* actress.

"No, I'm not her," she said. "But I want to be."

His attention dissolved. "So does everyone else, kid. Beat it."

She took a step nearer, eyes wide and hopeful. "But isn't this Maurice Steele's car?"

"Yeah, so."

She giggled. "I was hoping to have a chance to speak with Mr. Steele." What she wanted was the driver, a man Maurice kept waiting for his beck and call, to give up some details. Old ones.

"Send him your portfolio."

Clearly, he wasn't interested. She had to make him want her, then. "I have, but I need the edge, *n'est-ce pas?*"

The driver, Mike something, she recalled, eyed her from shoes to hair.

"You sure look like his type."

"Really?" she said brightly, toying with her hair. "You think so?"

"Breathing is his type, lady." Then in a moment of concern he said, "You sure you want to be near this man? He could make or break you."

"I want him to make me."

"Oh yeah?" Clearly he thought it would be the latter choice.

She cocked her head. "You don't like him much, do you?" Her voice was sexy and smooth, her accent just enough to intrigue him.

"Baby, what's to like?"

"I heard he was tough, but very smart."

The driver scoffed, pitching his smoke.

"I'd do anything to get the chance to speak with him. Privately."

"What's anything?"

Darcy swayed up to the driver, letting her breasts and hips do the talking for her. She blushed, but the facial mask hid her embarrassment. She touched his arm, leaning into his side and whispering in his ear as if she were sharing an intimate secret.

"Oh *mon cheri,* what wouldn't I do." She could feel his muscles tighten and hoped his imagination was going wild. "And I'd do anything with someone who'd get me there." Her voice was breathy and a little sound worked in his throat.

"Thinking of the casting couch, are you?"

She glanced pointedly at the silver-gray limo and let that speak for her.

He arched an eyebrow, practically smacking his lips in anticipation.

The sun was setting and he checked his watch. Maurice loved long, slow dinners, Darcy knew. All she needed was enough time to get this guy to talk.

"He's with a director and a couple writers going over the last draft of a new script. He'll be there awhile."

They'll be there half the night, Darcy thought. "And that means what to you and me, *cheri?*"

He simply popped open the car door, and she climbed in. Through the window, she could see him checking the area, signaling to another driver before slipping inside with her. Darcy already had the mini-tape recorder in her purse turned on.

She sat primly on the velvet seat, remembering riding in this car to premieres, to appointments and dinners. Just as she remembered the ugly things Maurice had said to her while the soundproof glass was between them and the driver. Maurice thought he'd made her into a lady, that she wouldn't be anything without his personal touch. Well, he'd touched her all right, beating down her self-esteem so badly that she'd been a shell of who she was now.

The driver leaned toward her, and she couldn't let him get too familiar or he might sense the facial mask. It had taken her hours to get the look she wanted, suggestive of a certain celebrity's face, but not too alike.

He tossed the hat aside and pulled off his jacket. She scooted away.

He scowled. "You teasing me?"

"No, *cheri.*" She gave him an innocent look laced with seduction. "But I'm not playing with you till you can guarantee I get time with Mr. Steele."

"Honey, you can be in this car, waiting for him if you want. When we're done, of course."

Her stomach knotted, yet she plastered on a smile and crossed her legs. His gaze followed them up to her skirt hem. "Tell me about him first, because when I'm done with you, you won't have the energy to talk."

He grinned. "He's a prick."

Her eyebrows shot up.

"He uses people and you're better off not knowing him."

"Then why do you work for such a man?"

"Money." His gaze raked over her like a hungry wolf's. "And the women."

She behaved as if that last comment went right over her head. "But I met him once, a long time ago, three years I think. He was very sweet to me. I recognize this car."

He scowled. "I remember every person that's been in this car, lady."

"Oh, I wasn't *in* the car, I met him..." She chewed her lip provocatively, sliding closer to him and running her hand up his thigh, dangerously close to his crotch. He reached for her and with an odd tenderness, he touched her breast.

Darcy's skin crawled as she suffered through it. She needed information.

"When did you meet him?" Mike asked.

She spit out the date. "October twenty-first. I believe it was late afternoon. I thought he might audition me for his movie—the one that's coming out now—*Dead Game.*"

Mike stiffened, scowling. "That date sounds familiar. Were you at the studio, waiting?"

"*Oui,* I was."

"The man *never* changes his schedule, but that night he'd stopped by Studio Eight, back lot."

Studio Eight, Pegasus Studios? She knew that area. It was storage for special effects-stunt division.

"I remember because it was the only time he didn't have me hang around." The driver gave her a hot look. "Now I know why."

"Oh, *mais non*, he wasn't with me, not that way." Or she wouldn't be playing this game, dumb ass.

"If he was, he'd have had your skirts up, kid."

Darcy doubted that. "He only said hello, and that he had an appointment. Perhaps another woman, *oui?*"

"Hell if I know. I came back an hour later, but no one else was there but Steele. And he was pretty eager to leave and pissed that I was two minutes late. The man doesn't think that L.A. traffic applies to him." He frowned. "Forget him, come here." He pulled her onto his lap, shoving his hands under her skirt and cupping her behind. She moaned and wiggled appropriately, biting his neck and wanting to spit afterward. She ground onto his crotch, feeling him get hard, and knew she had to end this or be raped.

"Come on," he said, "you've got me hard enough to crack nuts."

Well wasn't that graphic. "If we have time, *cheri*, then why rush things?" She pulled his shirt free, running her hands up his chest, then shifted, straddling his hips and gave him her version of a lap dance. He pawed her. She had to get away before his mauling wrecked her disguise.

Darcy wanted to run like hell to the nearest shower.

"I wonder who Steele was waiting for, if not me?" she murmured. "All I can remember is that he was wearing a dark suit. Looking very handsome."

"Yeah, yeah, handsome, rich, and still a prick. And he wasn't wearing a suit." He stilled and frowned at her.

Before he wised up, Darcy quickly cupped him through his trousers, shaping his erection and dragging his mind into desire. He moaned, grinding her hand on him.

Men were so easy sometimes.

"Feel good, *cheri?*" she purred when he buried his face in her breasts. He was massaging them as if they were softballs, almost painfully, and she decided it was time to end this before he separated the facial mask from her breasts. She rose up, wrapped her arms seductively around his neck, pushing his head to the side. She pressed and squeezed and kept the pressure on. In a few seconds, his hands slowed to a stop, a few seconds more and he was out cold. She released him and sat back.

Thank you, Athena Academy.

The sleeper hold wasn't dangerous, just cut off air supply for a bit. He'd rouse in a few minutes. She checked his pulse, then righted her clothing before she searched him and the car for anything useful. She found a supply of condoms in the bar console and a couple scraps of paper, which she pocketed, then she stepped out of the limousine. The sun had set and the streets were lit with gas lamps, and she glanced back to where the three other drivers were gathered. They grinned at her and she put her fingers to her lips, giving them a sassy wink before walking off, behind swaying and boobs bouncing.

So, the studio was where Maurice had gone that night.

That was unusual. Maurice rarely stepped on a lot unless there was trouble on a film. And he was never around the Special Effects department because he had no reason to be. He had people who did that errand stuff for him.

She had to get a look at exactly what was stored in the area, though she recalled only one large warehouse with several garagelike doors.

She hailed a cab, the driver taking her past Maurice's production offices. She closed her eyes for a second, trying to recall the layout. While it had a side-alley rolling door to bring in equipment, Maurice's office was on the top floor. The entire top floor.

Darcy glanced back briefly. Anything Maurice wanted to keep secret would either be there or at the house, and going to the house was out of the question. The office she could hit later tonight. First she had to get on that lot and see what was there.

* * *

In the morning, Darcy took the tour of the studio with fifty other guests to sunny California. She'd dressed like a middle-aged tourist because in her natural state, she'd probably be recognized. A half hour into the tour, they were near the same lot where the driver had left Maurice. Slipping away from the group was easy. Once she was out of sight, she hid behind a giant metal storage box and stripped out of the cheap clothes, rolling down her jean pant legs and adjusting the plain top she wore beneath. She clipped on her old IDs, which she'd altered with a couple changes to the picture and name, then slung the bag on her shoulder. She started walking. People were filming two blocks away, but Darcy was interested only in this particular spot. She moved fast, knowing that security would find her if she was seen or made noise. They took the security on sets very seriously.

The tall, wide doors to the studio warehouse building were locked. She checked behind herself before she pulled out her lock-picking set and worked the padlock. In a minute, she was slipping inside. There was little inside beyond various size crates, barrels and rows of metal cylinders. The stunt crews used the CO_2 canisters for things like making a car roll over or lifting fake buildings off the ground to give the effect of earthquakes. Not as if they needed that around the San Andreas Fault, she thought cynically, moving into the dark.

She was in a restricted area. If she got caught, she'd be thrown in jail and Maurice would win. *So don't get caught,* she thought. With her penlight, she scanned the areas, the odor of chemicals floating in the air, making the back of her throat feel dry. Bitter. *What* is *that?* She checked the contents of a couple of drums, jotting down the names. The element names were unfamiliar and she'd have to check them on her computer later. The smells were making her a little dizzy.

What had brought Maurice *here* that night?

She moved to the back of the building just as one of the wide rolling doors scraped open. She lunged toward a corner, crouching behind drums as workers filed in, grabbing cartons and cables.

Oh, hell. Oh, hell. They'll find me.

A truck engine roared as the vehicle backed into the warehouse entrance, and the crew began loading it with supplies for stunts. There were about ten people moving in and out and Darcy considered staying right where she was till they were gone, but couldn't take the chance of anyone seeing the side-door lock was gone and trapping her inside. Workers moved toward her position, gathering supplies. Sweat trickled under her mask, and her heart pounded as they neared.

If they saw her bag, they'd immediately think she was stealing. Stealing explosive material was a crime. God, they'd find her clothes, know she wore a facial mask. Oh, crap.

They came closer, and she shoved the bag under a discarded wood pallet, then inched her way to the doors, waiting for attention to focus on the loading before slipping out.

Immediately, she backtracked behind them and grabbed a roll of heavy cable. She loaded it on the truck. No one spared her a second look. Being around them felt familiar, though back when she was hired for a movie, she'd worked in the makeup department and, if on location, out of a trailer. It had been a cushy job, with two assistants helping her.

"Hey, what the hell do you think you're doing?"

Darcy looked up, hefting the stack of boxes and trying to keep the fear out of her expression. "My job."

"This is a restricted area."

"Well, no shit," she said, showing her old IDs and praying he didn't look at the expiration dates. "Penn sent me over here for more blasting caps." Luckily Darcy had glimpsed the list needed for the stunts posted inside the truck bed and who would oversee them.

"Well, get out." The man shook his head, rubbed his mouth. "Christ, they let anyone around this stuff."

"I know, I know, blow us all to hell and it's your responsibility." She handed him the heavy stack of boxes, forcing him to take it. "Then I guess you need to do it or trust us."

The assistant shot her a hard look and pushed the box back into her arms. "Get moving and don't come in here without an escort."

Darcy shrugged, chewing gum she didn't have, and walked away, then deposited the cartons in the truck. As soon as she was out of sight, she kept walking and circumvented the building. She had to go back there to get her bag and to look again. She'd smelled something familiar, but couldn't put her finger on what it was. Or where she'd smelled it before. Could it be just a memory of a smell from a movie set?

The workers and set directors kept her from getting inside without being noticed. Unfortunately someone had closed the padlock on the side door. She hid till the trucks rolled away, then, pulling tools from a small black pouch strapped to her calf, she went to work picking the padlock again. The sounds of trucks and cars moving around made her heart shoot to her throat. Voices grew louder, moving closer. Her hands shook so hard she couldn't get the lock open. In one sharp moment, she took a calm breath and worked the lock. It sprang, and she darted inside, flattening against the wall.

She paused long enough to get her heart where it belonged, then flipped on her penlight. It was pitch-black but cool, air conditioners keeping the materials stable. She moved to the back, getting her bag first. Her head felt fuzzy, her limbs a little rubbery. She turned sharply, almost falling on a canister. It tipped and an odor rose up from beneath. The drum was leaking and she lurched back, staggering and reaching for anything to keep from falling. Her hand smacked on a crate and she held on.

I'm going to lose my breakfast, she thought, her mouth watering, bitterness burning the back of her throat. She was still, waiting for it to pass. But it didn't and she struggled to reach the door, praying no one had put the lock back on, and grabbed the knob. Her head pounded, not with pain but as if it were filled with cotton and needed more room. She slipped out the door, and it took several tries to close the padlock. Darcy walked away, her steps weaving.

Unable to go another foot, she sagged against the wall and breathed deeply. The fuzzy feeling started to clear, but the taste in her mouth was still there. She dug in her bag for a bottle of water and drank, thinking that was stupid. All those chemicals in there, she could have blown herself up.

She climbed to her feet, heading toward the entrance and hoping she made it to her hotel room before she passed out.

* * *

In her hotel room Darcy slept for an hour, and her head was clear when she woke. She ordered room service, called Megan and spoke to Charlie. He was sweet and silly, and having fun with Meg's neighbors' puppies. When Megan got back on the line she gave Darcy the rundown on the salon's business.

"I don't know what I'd do without you, Meg."

"You'd fall apart. I want a raise."

Darcy laughed softly. "Take it out of petty cash."

"Jack called here for you."

Darcy stilled. "Oh."

"He didn't seem surprised you were out of town for a couple days."

"He saw Charlie on TV, Meg."

"Oh, God." Darcy told her about the segment about Rainy.

"You didn't tell him more, did you?"

"I had to tell him I knew Rainy, because he knew he'd seen Charlie. But I didn't say more than I had to, and he left angry."

"Let's hope Jack keeps his mouth shut about it."

Fear streaked through her bloodstream, tightening her features. "Why wouldn't he?"

"Maurice had millions, Darcy, how much would he pay for information on you?"

"Jack wouldn't do that." Would he?

"Are you ready to trust your life with that?"

"No, I'm not." And it proved that she'd let Jack deep into her life when she shouldn't have. "I'll be home in two days. I'll talk to him."

"I'll take care of things here, Darcy, but please, watch your back and don't do anything stupid."

"This is all stupid, Meg, but I have to, you know that."

Or she'd be locked in this hell forever.

She hung up and sat on the bed, but that only lasted a few seconds. She turned on the TV, bit into a cold French fry from dinner, then flipped through channels.

Something caught her attention and she flipped back to the local news. There was a big press party at the Beverly Center for *Dead Game*—a fan show, stars appearing, signing autographs, doing interviews before the premiere Friday night. That meant Maurice would be there. And not in his office.

Chapter 6

Staring up at Maurice's offices, Darcy popped a piece of gum in her mouth to help the dryness. It was as if the moisture in her mouth shut off when she was nervous.

And she was. Under her clothes she wore a synthetic catsuit, skintight and unrestricting. She felt like Jane Bond about to infiltrate a death-squad hideout.

Armed with her knife, wire cutters and lock picks, she had black nylon rope wound around her waist, just in case she needed it. She didn't know why, but having it made her feel better when she knew she hadn't planned this well enough. She didn't have time, nor any way to access information other than city plans. For a second, she wished she'd asked Jack for more equipment, then instantly dismissed that— he was being nosy enough already.

Going through the front door was out of the question. The building had a guard at the desk and a security system. Maurice had boasted about it once, as if warning her that there was a part of his life she would never know.

She knew enough. She checked the lower window, finding metal-strip sensors on the glass and locks. Okay that wasn't an option. Think. She could feel the clock ticking away her chances.

The pre-premiere party was for the staff, crew, actors and sponsors and would go on all night. Maurice would make a graceful escape soon enough, though she doubted he'd come back here anyway. But she didn't want to risk it.

She circled to the back, her gaze traveling up the art-deco line of the building that used to house the offices of Edgar Bergen. Surprisingly there wasn't a fire-escape ladder that reached past the third floor. She had to scale the building. Stripping off her jeans and shirt and leaving them in a ball by the trash, she grasped the end of a brick indentation and pulled herself up, glancing down to check the area again. She looked to the top.

Man, it was far. If she fell, she'd be a flying Wallenda trapeze artist without a net.

She hooked her toes in the brick work, taking her time, breathing slowly. In her training at Athena, they'd scaled rock walls and, as she moved, everything Rainy and her instructors had taught her came rushing back. Secure the footing first, don't overreach.

I can do this. Energy surged, her confidence building as she passed the third floor. Her aim was the roof. The buildings weren't close enough for her to risk jumping from one to the other from the top floors. Besides, the neighboring building was only three floors tall. She was in good shape, just not that good. She stretched her arms, her feet braced on the sill of an office window. If she remembered right, it was the bathroom. Even that had a sensor and she was careful not to touch it with her foot.

Darcy held on, her hands sweating, her toes curling to grip. She stretched again to reach the next brick. They stuck out at different spots, creating a pattern of sweeping curls in the wall. *One more, don't rush it.*

Cars moved past on the street, voices, faint and distant, pierced the night's silence.

Carefully she pulled her leg up, using her toes to feel the wall. When she found purchase, she pushed.

And slipped.

Her chin hit the brick and her muscles seized. She clutched the brick hard. Her breathing rushed with quick panic, and she was suddenly mad that she'd been brought to this.

Darcy struggled for five more minutes, choosing each move carefully, her fear replaced with tenacity. When she reached the top she grasped the edge, dangling like a noodle, then used her arms to pull herself up.

She swung her leg over the edge and hiked herself onto the roof. For a second, she just stayed there on her knees, catching her breath. Then she stood, looking around.

Air vents. Fire door. Glass skylight to Maurice's sitting area. She moved to that, looking down.

The room below looked opaque, the shapes undefinable. She reached for the lock, stopping short when she saw the metal tape. She unwound the rope, leaving it behind, and moved to the vents. She didn't bother pulling one apart, they were too narrow. Her hips would never fit through, and she didn't know where they led.

She went to the fire door and checked it for sensors. There weren't any. She frowned at that, double-checking, then slipping on latex gloves, she knelt, put her penlight in her mouth and used her picks to open the lock. Her hands grew slippery with sweat inside the gloves. She expected the alarm to sound.

The lock sprang. She slipped inside, padding down the short staircase that ran to the first floor right outside the guard's desk. She moved quietly, knowing sound would echo down the narrow stairwell and alert the guard. Who was armed.

She pushed open the door to Maurice's floor.

The hall was dark, the carpet lush and new smelling. What little moonlight there was coming through the open doors reflected off the pictures that lined the walls, shots of Maurice with actors and directors, and promo posters of movies.

Surrounded by all your glory, eh, Maurice?

She moved down the hall, silent, slow, then went into her husband's office. There was no reason for him to lock the door. No one came on this floor unless he said so.

She shined her light over the room, which stretched the length of the building, decorated for masculine power and money. Darcy spotted several new pieces of art, a leather-sofa grouping to the left, a sparkling wet bar behind that near the window. In the center, the skylight reflected the black surface of a small conference table before his desk.

Like a king holding court.

In a small room to her far left were copiers, fax machines and a bathroom complete with a shower and a closet.

Darcy went right to the files in the Brazilian mahogany cabinets behind the desk. She flipped through them, looking for anything on taxes, financial reports that would connect Maurice and

Porche. And mostly anything that was dated and signed after Fairchild had vanished. When she didn't come across anything, she grew antsy, a little dispirited.

He had to have it here. He'd need it for his accountants.

A sliver of hopelessness pierced her and she sighed, sitting in his chair. The leather was so cold she felt it through the cat suit. Her gaze fell on his computer and she turned on the screen. With the mouse, she opened files, reading quickly. Nothing. Leaving the desk, she moved her penlight over the room's interior.

She studied the bookcases, four wide and lining the wall opposite the desk. She barely noted the titles till she realized the same sets of books were on two shelves. She tipped a few out, then back, going down the line. It wasn't until she reached the third row that she found it. A little switch. She flicked it. The wall sprang with a soft sigh.

Very clever, Maurice, very clever.

Behind it was a safe.

Hell.

That didn't do her much good. She couldn't open it.

A lock, sure, but a safe?

She tried anyway, using his birthday, then their wedding day. The day his first film was released. Maurice had trouble remembering sequences of numbers, so he kept them familiar. It was how she'd gotten into his personal finances through the online search.

She dropped her arms, staring at the unopened safe.

Nothing worked.

She checked her watch, aware she was running out of time. She gave it one last try, and for reasons she couldn't say, she tried Charlie's birth date.

It clicked open.

Darcy blinked, stunned to her soles.

Maurice using Charlie's birthday when he'd pushed her down the stairs to make her lose him? When he'd ignored her son when Charlie was born?

It didn't please her.

It made her more afraid.

Because it meant that, no matter what Maurice had said or done, Charlie was important to him. She didn't want that. She wanted her son for herself. God, she didn't want Maurice even thinking about him!

Shaking off this new concern till later, she rose on her toes and peered in, then lifted out the stacks of paper. She found cash bound in ten-grand increments, bonds and his passport. And hers. She considered taking it, but then he'd know she was here. Yet she stared at the picture, seeing a stylish woman, sapphires dangling from her ears to match her suit. She snapped it closed.

That Darcy was dead.

She brought the stack to the floor, spreading it out. She expected to find computer discs of information, but it was all paper. She flipped and read, careful to keep the papers aligned as they were. Then she found what she needed and felt almost giddy. The final documents of the loan for the production.

She didn't see a thing wrong with them, though by the graininess at the top of the page, she could tell they were copies. Porche would have the original to file with the banking commission. She hurried to the copier near the bathroom, shut the door and started the machine. It sighed softly as each scan-and-copy printed and she peeked out the door, wondering if the guard made nightly rounds. She checked her watch. Damn. It was fast approaching midnight.

Darcy willed the copier to move faster, then glanced at the immaculate bathroom, the small open closet outside hung with two suits and fresh shirts. She searched the pockets, finding nothing but cleaner stubs and the monogramming order.

The copying done, she rolled hers into a tube and went back to the safe to replace the others, stacking everything exactly as it had been and putting them back in the safe.

Returning the wall to its closed position, she grabbed a rubber band from the desk to secure the tube of papers and headed to the door. She was nearly there when she stilled, hearing something. It took her about two seconds for the sound of a knob turning to register.

Oh, no.

She turned back, ducking behind the four-foot-wide wall that sectioned the office from the conference area. She went motionless, her breathing light and slow. She didn't hear footsteps or keys. Then the door opened sharply, a wide beam of light glazing over the room. She could almost feel a figure approaching, hear his breathing. Oh, man, oh, man.

Darcy held her breath. The light speared over the interior, then clicked off.

She still didn't move, waiting for her heart to slow down, then she checked her watch. Midnight on the dot. She stayed where she was till she heard the close of a door somewhere down the hall, then moved to the door, wondering how she'd get down from here and what to do next.

She needed to lure Maurice, scare him a little to see if she was on the right track. She stopped and turned back.

She knew just how to do it.

Leaning over his chair, she opened the Web browser on his computer. The high-speed line was open and she went to Yahoo.com and sent a blind message.

I'm back. 11 PM, lot 8.
P.F.

That should do it.

She deleted the cookies and history, then dumped the trash bin, erasing her trail. It was a long shot, but he lived by e-mail, voice mail and cell phones. And she didn't have any time left. She repositioned everything on the desk, including the chair. Maurice's world was a precise and orderly one. It almost made him predictable.

Darcy headed out, careful to close the doors without a sound. On the roof, she looked down at the ground, and decided against using the rope. She'd no way to release it and it would leave a trail. She went over the edge, working her way down. She ran toward her car, parked several blocks down behind a store, careful to stay in the shadows.

If Maurice showed tomorrow night, he was guilty.

Because if he wasn't, he wouldn't bother, nor would he understand the message.

One thing she knew about her husband was that he wouldn't waste time on someone who didn't have the power to take him down.

The following evening, Darcy strolled through the Pegasus Studio gates, smiling at the guard and showing her ID. She'd reconstructed the ID today using a five-minute photo taken in a machine in a drugstore. To the guard she was a young man in jeans and a jacket, so she didn't offer more than a couple of grunts. Her mask was broader and whiskered, her hair hidden beneath a tight wig. While her waist was straighter with padding and her breasts were smashed under Ace bandages, it was the socks in her crotch that itched. But it wouldn't do to have nothing there. She sort of understood guys' need to adjust themselves all the time.

It was nearly ten-thirty and the guard was more interested in checking the time than looking closely at her ID. His relief must be coming, she thought, finally passing through and walking toward the lights set up on the lot for night filming. The area was quiet, almost ghostly, and when she was out of sight of the guards, she veered right, quickly moving down the alleys between buildings. Most of the buildings near the roads were for shows where the public could watch the taping, but farther to the west was storage. The warehouse where the chauffeur said Maurice had gone that night. She picked the padlock, leaving it discreetly open.

A little piece of bait.

Darcy had been there that morning, searching for the best point to see activity and the least likely place to be spotted. The roof was her best option, but she hadn't had time in the daylight to set anything up without looking suspicious.

Her gaze landed on the fire-escape ladder on the building across the street and she stepped under it, hopping to give it a tug. It didn't move down. Probably rusted into position. Yet if it slid to the ground as it was supposed to, the noise would alert anyone within half a mile.

No guts, no glory, she thought, adjusting her backpack before she jumped, grabbing the rung. It squeaked and she dangled for a second, then reached for the next rung, swinging her leg upward till her foot caught a bar and took some of her weight so she could ease up to reach the next rung. The thing creaked with every move and she looked around, then pulled her body weight up two more before her feet connected solidly with the medal step. She climbed, looking back to see if any cars were coming, then threw herself over the ledge of the flat roof.

It didn't feel very stable under her feet, almost soft, and she crouched near the edge, shifting carefully to get the best view of the doors, the road and anything nearby. From the backpack she removed the night-vision goggles she'd bought at a pawnshop several months back and Jack's video camera, flipping the night-vision lens into place, then setting the camera on motion sensor. She propped it on her backpack a few feet to her right, sighted in, then with the NVGs she settled in to wait.

He'd show. He was in this up to his Armani lapels and gold collar stays. The next ten minutes stretched her nerves, every creak making her think she'd be discovered or the roof would give out under her.

She could see the headline. Studio Collapses, Leaves Kidnapping Mother Under Ten Tons Of Rubble. Child Unaccounted For. She'd rather it said Movie Mogul Maurice Steele Indicted For Murder. She spent the next five minutes creating headlines that lightened her mood until she heard the crunch of gravel. Then the sound of a car engine.

Sighting in with the NVGs, she peered over the edge of the roofline. A dark sedan moved up the alley, and she focused on the license plate.

FLM MKR. Short for filmmaker.

Well, Maury, honey, you didn't trust your driver with this, did you?

The car moved slowly and from her position she couldn't see the driver. Besides, the windows were tinted. She glanced to the right to check the video camera. It was filming. Her palms went clammy, and adrenaline rushed in her veins, speeding up her heartbeat as she waited for the driver to stop and get out. Seconds passed. The car rolled, the crush of gravel beneath the tires loud and intrusive.

The car door opened and Darcy almost squeaked

when Maurice stepped out. He left the lights on, the car running and the door open. *Thinking you'll need a quick getaway?* Maurice waited, rubbing his mouth, pacing, cursing, the same behavior he'd had that night. He was rarely nervous, so it always stood out more.

He moved in front of the headlights and Darcy reared back at the clothing he wore. Jeans, which he wouldn't have been caught dead wearing otherwise, a T-shirt and a shabby tweed jacket. So un-Maury. Did he think that was a disguise? Where'd he get that, Goodwill?

He moved to the warehouse door, trying the lock and when he realized it was open he let it go, stepping back, shocked. Something moved, a rat probably, but enough to make a scraping sound.

Maurice whipped around. *Oh, God,* she mouthed when he pulled a small gun from behind his back. Maurice moved to the next door a few yards to the left, peering through the wire-reinforced glass window. *What's in there, Maury? The body? The weapon?* Darcy hadn't seen any evidence to say so when she was in there the other day, but it would have been easy to hide—drop the body into one of the barrel tanks or drums, seal it up and the body would decompose with the strength of the chemicals. Half of them were blends with sulfuric acid.

Clever.

He looked around, then he disappeared down the narrow corridor between the buildings, big enough for a person to walk down but not enough for a vehicle.

Darcy waited, not daring to move. One tiny scrape would echo and alert him. He had a gun, she just had her knife.

When he reappeared, he went to the door, removing the lock and pocketing it before he pried the door open. It was a nearly airtight seal and the pop was loud. The reason Darcy hadn't tried it tonight.

Maurice didn't seem to care. He walked inside, and Darcy shifted farther to her right for a better angle, getting a bird's-eye view of the entrance and a few yards inside. Maurice went to the left. To the back. She saw his shadow pass by the only window in the place.

If he was used to skulking he'd have known he'd cast a shadow.

And he didn't wear gloves. She made a note of everything he touched that she could see and didn't wonder what he was doing. He was implicating himself by being there. He didn't turn on a light or use a flashlight. That meant he knew his way around. Or exactly where he'd been.

Less than two minutes later he came out, closed the door and put the lock back on. With a silk handkerchief, he wiped off his prints. Then he pulled out his cell phone and dialed.

"Did you find out who sent that message?"

He must be talking to his secretary, Alisha Watts.

Alisha was hardworking, always a step ahead of Maurice, and a long time ago, she'd been Darcy's friend. She also knew the darker side of Maurice, the side he never showed to the public. Darcy hadn't asked Alisha for help years ago—Alisha needed her job to support her daughter—yet she'd won Darcy's eternal gratitude when she'd called to say Maurice was out of the city till very late. Darcy had phoned Rainy that night and disappeared.

"Well try harder, dammit. Your job is on the line, Ms. Watts."

A lie. Maurice couldn't function without Alisha and since she'd been trying to get Maurice to promote her for years now, without success, she wouldn't put forth a whole lot of effort for an "undisclosed sender" message.

"I don't need to be pulled out of meetings for crap like this."

Meetings, my fanny, she thought, studying him. She could almost tick off the seconds before he exploded. He cut the call and dialed another. From the gist of the conversation he was talking to a lawyer.

Darcy smiled. He was scared. Maurice *was* a lawyer.

"It's got to be someone who saw that damn TV

segment mentioning Fairchild and is looking for some easy cash."

He listened then said, "Hell, no, I'm not offering or paying. I just want the little bastard. No, no, you saw the loan papers. You approved them. What am I paying you for, Crommer, if not to watch my back? Fine, fine. You know good and well that Fairchild is in Europe living off the profits I made for her! If she wants to hide like a hobbit, what do I care?"

Darcy could almost see the noose squeezing his tanned neck. He hung up, then moved to the car, standing between the car and the open door. He looked around, looked up to where she was perched. Darcy hunched.

"I don't know what you want," Maurice called out softly, foolishly. "But you won't get it."

Really, she thought, wishing she had a rifle. With a nightscope. Silencer, too. Of course, it would be nice, if she actually had the guts to shoot a human being, that would probably help.

Darcy knew her limits. She wasn't a killer.

But she might have married one.

He climbed into the car, backing out.

Darcy leaned against the lip of the building and for a moment stared up at the stars, considering all she'd accomplished and whether or not this trip would evolve into more. She'd have to go over the financial reports, dig for more. She had documents signed by Fairchild, but she'd need some handwriting samples to compare.

Later, she thought, reaching for the camera and backpack.

It was time to go home.

Chapter 7

Darcy did a hip-grinding walk on her way across the salon to some kicking Nelly Furtado music, shaking the application bottle of tint for Liza Ringling. The success of her trip to Hollywood gave her extra energy and her clients were feeling it.

The joint was jumping. Blow-dryers whined and chatter filled the space in the air. Charlie was in the corner, his own private spot, nodding his head to the music and playing with his toys. *I've got a great kid,* she thought, smiling at him when he squished his nose at her.

Megan was at the appointment desk, her dark hair twisted up in chopsticks and her long, thin legs propped on a stool. She deserved the break. She'd been Darcy's right hand and sometimes her left since Rainy had died.

The customers were enjoying the late-afternoon jam session and most were getting the full treatment. Her Korean manicure-pedicurist chatted away in heavily accented English, and the masseur was escorting Rayleen Pickman to the private room. The schoolteacher would love the soft music during the warm-oil massage, and the chance to feel pampered. Chasing after thirty six-year-olds couldn't be easy. Darcy glanced at the tanning booth, checking the timer. She had a client in there trying to maintain her summer tan. But then, Sue Ash was eighteen, beautiful, with a body every boy in town was panting after. A tan would make little difference.

Full service, she thought, grinding to Furtado and tinting light brown hair red.

"You think he'll like it?" Liza asked nervously.

Darcy met her gaze in the chrome-rimmed mirror. Liza's husband was going to love it, she thought. "Every man wants a redhead once in a while. Makes him think he's walking on the wild side. Besides, if you don't like it, I'll tint it back for free. But you have to wait at least two weeks." Though not one customer had ever asked to be tinted back to their original color. "Dark red hair, a kicky new cut—Dave will think he's sleeping with another woman."

"Well heck, he can't argue with that," Liza said. "A consenting affair?"

"The best kind," Darcy said, and Jack, all tight T-shirt and rippling muscles flashed in her mind. Quickly she pushed him out and suggested Liza pop over to the lingerie shop and give her husband more of a treat. She finished applying the color, snapped off her gloves and set the timer. Giving Liza a nudge, she handed her the latest trendy lingerie catalogue before she went off to get the woman her favorite mocha latte.

In the supply room, she'd just finished making the drink when Meg came in, holding the cordless phone.

"It's Alexandra Forsythe," she said softly and Darcy stilled, then handed the fat mug over to Meg.

"That's for Liza, let me know when the timer goes off," she said, taking the phone.

Meg frowned, pulling the door closed.

"Alex, hey, girl."

"Hello, Darcy, how's that handsome three-foot man of yours?"

"He's great. Wish I could bottle his energy. So what's up?"

"I called to tell you that I met the Dark Angel."

"Oh my God." The Dark Angel was a legendary figure at Athena Academy. Years ago, he'd broken into the school and accused the Academy of killing his sister. A few students, including Alex, had caught a glimpse of the handsome, passionate youth. The legend had started there and was still making the rounds among students today.

"My thoughts exactly at the time. Remember the FBI agent I caught snooping around Athena Academy? His name is Justin Cohen."

Alex had told Darcy, Kayla and Tory about catching him at the school. She also thought she'd spotted him at Rainy's funeral. "So what was he up to all those years ago breaking into Athena and causing hell?"

"He was trying to find a connection to his sister Kelly's death. He thought that Athena had something to do with it."

That didn't make sense. "Wait a sec, back up and start over."

"I know, it sounds strange, but given what we know about the egg harvesting and Rainy's ovaries being scarred and the accident, it's not that far off. His sister became a surrogate mother around the time of Rainy's supposed appendectomy. Her doctor was Dr. Henry Reagan, the man who signed off on Rainy's chart. And Dr. Reagan's part-time nurse was our own Betsy Stone."

"Oh hell." Betsy Stone was Athena Academy's nurse.

"His sister died during the birth and the hospital records show that the baby died along with her."

"But you don't believe it?"

"No."

"I'm with you. If the mother was dying, they'd have tried to save the baby before that, and if she was a surrogate, someone was probably paying big bucks for that child."

"I concur," Alex said and Darcy smiled. Alexandra Forsythe was old money, highly educated, a "came over on the Mayflower" blue blood, and the furthest thing from a rich snot that there was. But sometimes that upbringing showed in her speech.

"Where is Dr. Reagan now?"

"Justin learned that he died of a heart attack years ago. Kayla is trying to track down his files. Justin's been keeping track of Athena Academy all these years. When he heard about Rainy's accident, he checked it out and realized that we all suspected it was murder."

"We know she was murdered, we just have to prove it."

There was silence for a second or two, and Darcy knew that the suspicions cast on Athena Academy had shattered the very foundation of Alex's upbringing. Her family had helped to found Athena Academy.

The evidence they had pointed right to the Academy and Betsy Stone. But was she in on it? Or had someone used Betsy to get to the school? They had to be careful about questioning the nurse. If she got spooked and took off, they'd be back to square one. Finding out exactly who else was involved and why without ruining the school's reputation was going to be a tough act to play. "What can I do?"

"Kayla mentioned that you were doing some private investigative work."

"I'm still learning really." Firsthand, she thought. The skills came in handy when she was rescuing women from their abusers. But the Cassandras didn't know about that. Yet. "You don't want to use your FBI connections to hunt, do you?"

"No, this is personal. And I'd rather keep this between those I trust."

Darcy smiled, touched. "You want me to check out the surrogate-mother angle? Won't be easy. The trail is twenty years old but I'd bet if there was one, then there were more."

"I agree, Kayla's running a search at Athena for possible leads and we're still looking for the fertility specialist Rainy was seeing just before her death, Dr. Deborah Halburg."

Still? Where could the woman be? "I'll get right on it. Alex, does Justin know about the egg mining?"

"No. We really don't have enough information yet. But he wants to work with us on the investigation. I…think it might be a good plan." Something in Alex's voice sounded odd. Had the renegade Dark Angel gotten under her usually reserved skin? Darcy suspected as much when Alex abruptly changed the subject. "And by the way, I had a car accident."

"What? Oh, my God! Were you hurt? When was this? What happened?"

"Darcy."

"Yes?"

"Take a breath."

She did, slowly. "Jeez, you must be okay if you're that matter-of-fact about it."

"I'm fine, nothing major—but I passed out while driving."

"Like Kayla did on the Athena grounds?" Kayla had been searching for Rainy's Athena medical files when she fainted dead away for no apparent reason, too.

"I believe so."

That was three people. Rainy falling asleep at the wheel and dying. Kayla. And now Alex. "That's no longer a coincidence, Alex."

"I agree. My doctor said there was nothing wrong with me to make me faint."

"This is getting dangerous. Someone doesn't want us getting any closer to the truth."

"I will use every caution. And so should you."

There was a knock on the door and Meg peered inside, pointing to her head. "I hate to cut you off, but I've got to get back to work. I'll let you know what I turn up as soon as I have something."

"Thanks, Darcy. And Darcy…" Alex seemed suddenly hesitant. It wasn't like her. "If you need any help, for…anything at all, you know I'm here for you, too. We all are."

Darcy's throat closed a little. She knew her friends had known something was going on with her when they'd seen her dyed hair at the funeral. It hadn't been the time to talk, but her friend's concern touched her. "Thanks, Alex. I'll let you know." She started to hang up then said, "Oh, wait a sec. This FBI agent, aka our illustrious Dark Angel…is he as handsome as we all imagined him to be?"

"Oh, yes."

Darcy grinned. She'd been right. She could almost feel the sparks shooting through the phone. "Talk to you later. Stay cool, Alex." Darcy could hear Alex chuckle as she hung up.

She tapped the phone against her thigh for a second, thinking. Three women from Athena had fainted for no reason. One had died because of it. And Betsy Stone? What did she have to do with all this? Being the Academy's nurse she had access to a lot of personal information, including medical and administrative records and medications. And Darcy would bet she knew when the girls had their cycles. Stone kept the supplies.

Darcy shook her head, worried about her friends as she went back to Liza and turned an understated beauty into a knockout with rich, red hair.

Sitting at a wide glass table on the back patio, Maurice Steele propped his feet on a chair, slipped on his sunglasses, then sipped his morning coffee. The water in the pool glistened like diamonds in the bright morning sun. A soft ocean breeze flicked at the wide Panama umbrella overhead and mussed his hair. He smoothed it back, reading the newspaper, making notes and ignoring the incident of the night before. Someone was jerking his chain and he felt foolish for responding.

And he hated feeling foolish, even if no one saw it.

A small TV perched on a table a couple feet away reported the news, but Maurice was interested only in the stack of newspapers in front of him and what they said about him and the movie that had premiered the other night. He went straight to the reviews, scanning them quickly and picked out small phrases that pumped his blood pressure. *Excellent. Five star, tremendously crafted script. Perfect for the role. Stellar performance.*

I told them. They hadn't believed him. He could see his bank accounts filling as his prestige and clout grew. *Now they'll come begging.*

He glanced at the screen, seeing Fairchild's face on the TV, then his. Christ. They pay attention to that drivel when the biggest blockbuster movie of the year just hit theaters? People were hanging out overnight to be the first to see it. "Report on that," he snapped at the TV anchor who looked too much like a playboy bunny and not enough like a professional. What was her name, Shannon Conner?

He smiled. She was the reporter who'd done the exposé on Athena Academy and inadvertently given him the means to hunt down his errant wife. He liked her better already.

I could change your life, he thought, seeing the woman with slightly darker hair, a less revealing suit. *And for God's sake, get rid of those earrings. They look like the Eiffel Tower.*

He'd made thousands over so they were appealing to the world. As he'd done for himself. He'd rewritten his own past, carved away the barrio and replaced it with Bel Air. He'd watched and learned, working two, sometimes three jobs, making himself indispensable to the people who had the power, clawing his way between them. He knew he'd used people, been cruel and conniving. But he'd have done anything not to be trapped in an L.A. gang and walk with a homeboy hump in his step.

Manny Sanchez was Maurice Steele.

No one knew.

He'd paid a fortune to have it erased. He was proud of what he'd accomplished, he thought, sipping his coffee.

He spun straw into gold now.

Maurice looked around at his home, the ocean crashing a few hundred yards away while the clear water of the pool rippled. The best of both. In his mind he saw his wife backstroking through the water, her slim body a tanned torpedo as she flipped and swam back. She rested her arms on the edge of the pool, smiled at him.

Something sharpened in his chest.

His weakness was her, he supposed, pinching the bridge of his nose. She was the only woman who could make him hurt.

No longer interested in spending time alone, he left the lanai and marched upstairs to his bedroom. Instantly his gaze fell on the real naked woman in his bed. Her breasts were plump—and, a surprise, real. Blond hair was mussed and long, her face elfin and dainty. Suddenly, he didn't see the aspiring actress, he saw Darcy, bare and open for him.

He moved toward the bed, untying his robe.

She stirred and rolled over, dazed with confusion till the memory of last night played across her face. He'd taken her home from the premiere.

"Hi," she said softly, smiling and reaching for him.

"Ah, my love." He lay over her, pushing her legs

apart, and in an instant he thrust into her, whispering another woman's name.

Darcy tapped the keys, searching through archives of old newspapers in Arizona and Nevada. Athena Academy was near Phoenix, so anything in the outlying areas could be a source. It would take a while, she thought and glanced at the clock. She had five minutes before her next client arrived. This was her fifth search in two days for anything suspicious. She'd read through everything from penny savers to tourist magazines, looking for something that could be construed as an ad for a surrogate. She had five possible ads but she needed to narrow the search. She considered placing her own ad, offering a reward for information. Money always drew the real nutcases, but she'd know what to ask to make certain she was on the right track.

Her five minutes up, she stood, glancing at her notes from her L.A. trip and feeling torn between devoting her time to searching for the surrogate and following up on the details from her trip. She still had to research the names of the chemicals she'd seen on the barrels in the warehouse and dig out the freezer bags to see what else she could learn. Plus she was waiting for Porche's assistant, Marianna Vasquez, to call her back. She'd made another call to the woman, wishing she'd had the time in L.A. to meet with her face-to-face.

She headed back into the salon, stopping by the extra room to check on Charlie. He was still napping and she bent to kiss his cool cheek. He wiggled deeper into the covers. He'd be in preschool soon, then first grade. She had to get her life back to normal before then. She couldn't register him for school under an alias. And well, Charlie Daniels drew a lot of attention. Darcy hadn't thought of that when she chose her alias. Charlie had been a baby at the time. She smiled. Stupid but funny, she thought. Now she was stuck with it.

She moved into the main salon, glad it was on the edge of town, far enough from street traffic but close enough to do a good walk-in business. There was a shop on either side of hers, and the facades were all designed to look like Old Western storefronts. She had a clear view of the street traffic from all sides and the backyard was big enough for Charlie to have some fun. Her own house was just two lots back, a one-story small bungalow style just big enough for her and Charlie. Megan lived at the other end of town, which didn't say much, since she was only a couple miles away.

Darcy gathered up towels and grabbed a trash can to empty. One of her stylists, Nicki, flashed her a thank-you smile. She was young and pretty, her belly ring showing above low-riding capri slacks and shoes stacked so high Darcy waited for the nose bleed to start. Lana had the next chair, and was fresh out of cosmetology school, but Darcy had spotted talent. The eighteen-year-old was apprenticing under Darcy, yet the girl could cut hair in half the time of the rest and therefore made more money. Shianne and Zoe worked side by side, the best of pals. Shianne was tiny and blonde, and Zoe was tall with hair the color of bing cherries. The manicurist and masseur showed up when they had appointments and weren't in today. Although the salon was filled with customers, no one was waiting for someone's time. The mood was soft and quiet, and Darcy slipped in a Nora Jones CD and let the sexy jazz move through the place like smoke.

Darcy emptied the trash, started a load of towels, then swept the floors, checking her watch for her next client.

The noise level lowered suddenly and Nicki called to her. "I think your next client is here."

Darcy set the broom aside, coming around the bend that hid the shampoo bowls from public view, then stopping dead in her tracks.

Oh be still my wicked heart, she thought, and for a second she just appreciated the good-looking man.

He had one arm braced on the windshield of the appointment desk, talking with Megan. Who, Darcy noticed, was practically melting into a puddle in the bucket car seat that served as a chair. Whatever he was saying was making Meg blush. She glanced at the other stylists. The girls and her customers had stopped to stare. Darcy waved at them to get back to work and not embarrass themselves. Nicki shifted a couple steps closer.

"Is he just too yummy or what? He looks like something out of an L.L. Bean catalogue."

"Yeah," Darcy said. "He does have that handsome outdoorsy look, huh?"

Nicki gave her a nudge. "He's your appointment, you lucky girl."

Darcy moved nearer, thinking that tall, blond and handsome looked like he could climb a rock face or trek through Nepal with ease. His buff-colored Adirondack-style jacket with pockets and pull cords looked right on him, and he had it pushed back with his fist braced on his hip. Long legs in jeans ended in Timberline boots.

"Hello," she said, and when he turned his attention, the most beautiful pair of blue eyes locked on her.

"Please tell me you're Piper."

He's English, she realized, his accent educated, soft. James-Bond sexy. "I am."

He excused himself from Meg, then moved toward Darcy. "I'm Kel Adams."

His gaze moved over her from head to toe, making her conscious of everything from her exposed tummy to how her breasts sat in her bra.

"Thank you for the last-minute appointment."

"No problem." Her gaze moved to his hair. "Looks like you need it."

"Yes, a good shearing more likely." He ruffled his long, shaggy blond hair. "I've been in the Australian outback for a couple months and didn't have time before my—" He stopped, then let out a long-suffering sigh. "Forgive me, making excuses again."

"Something you and your therapist are working on?"

He cast her a devilish look that made her insides light up and shimmer.

"No. I chatter a bit much on useless things, though. Has a tendency to irritate some people. Rather like listening to an excited five-year-old, I'm told."

"Then you'll fit in here." She inclined her head toward the back. "Let's shampoo first."

Kel nodded, following her. Snapping on the cap and wetting his hair, Darcy could smell his aftershave. There was something about having an attractive man staring directly at your breasts that wasn't the least bit businesslike.

He closed his eyes, and as she shampooed and rinsed, he moaned softly.

"Sorry. Could have gone to sleep right then."

"I get that a lot."

He chuckled, sitting up, and she rubbed the towel over his hair, then ignored the puppy-dog way he looked up at her. "Wonderful view."

Her face reddened and she escorted him to her chair, thinking that he was at least making a boring day better. She turned him toward the mirror.

"How would you like it trimmed?"

"Been hacking at it myself lately, so you be the judge."

"Ah, a trusting nature," she said, wiggling her eyebrows and opening and closing her scissors viciously.

"You're the professional."

Darcy stared at his reflection, judging facial structure, length, then started. Kel was a photographer, she learned, in town to get some Old-West-style shots of houses and old buildings.

Kel was easygoing, less inclined to get into a heavy discussion and more into teasing them all. "Men should come in here just for the view."

"As long as they pay, we don't care, do we, ladies?"

The air was peppered with agreements and long looks at the handsome Brit.

"Stop moving or I'll make a noticeable hole in your hair."

He shrugged. "It will grow back."

He flirted like a teenager, with innuendoes and sly infectious smiles. When she was finished, she decided he looked even better than before. He paid, left her too big a tip and said "Cheers" as he walked out. Half her staff leaned out to watch him go.

Darcy couldn't help joining them as he swung onto a motorcycle and drove off. A couple minutes later, though, he was right back, jumping off and rushing inside.

"Forget something, Kel?"

He walked straight toward her, stopping just two feet away. "Go out with me, Piper."

Darcy stilled, staring blankly. "I don't think so."

"Why? You don't like the accent? Charms the ladies all the time." He winked at Nicki. "Though my mother would say I've the poorest diction in all of Christendom."

"Mothers like to needle. And I don't date customers."

"You don't date at all," Nicki said and Darcy sent her a "butt out" look.

His gaze raked her slim body. "Pity. How about dinner?"

"I'm not interested in a relationship." She thought of Jack. Though theirs was a strange friendship, it was close enough to a relationship that she didn't want more of one till her life was in order.

Kel's expression went soft. "It's just dinner, love." He inched closer, his gaze locked with hers.

Darcy felt pressured, though she did want to go out, just for fun. And she was so tired of her own company. Before she made the decision, Charlie wandered out. She excused herself, gathering her son in her arms. He was still groggy from his nap, and she kissed his cheek, then set him in her chair.

"Hi," he said to Kel, knuckling his eyes.

"Hi yourself, lad."

"I'm Charlie. You talk funny."

"That's because I'm English, you know, the mother tongue."

Charlie made a face and Darcy nudged Kel. "Wit is lost on a three-year-old."

"Apparently."

"What are you doing with my mom's tongue?" Charlie asked, and barely muffled snickers filled the salon.

"Nothing...yet."

"Kel."

Laughing to himself, he said, "Ah, he's an adorable child, Piper."

"Thanks, and he remembers everything, so be careful what you say."

"I've noticed. So, Charles, have you been to that park, the one near the stockyards?"

Charlie was suddenly wide-awake and shifting to his knees. "The one with the *really* big Ferris wheel?"

"I believe so, yes."

"Nope." He sank into the chair. "Mom says I'm too small."

"You look the right size to me."

Charlie glanced at his mother accusingly. "Mom says, soon."

Kel twisted to look back at Darcy. "How about the park, Piper, with Charlie, tomorrow night? Popcorn, cotton candy, greasy American hot dogs?"

"Well, that was very manipulative of you."

He just kept grinning. "And they say the English are stodgy."

"Don't you have to work?"

"Can't shoot film in the dark. Lost half my lighting equipment between here and Sydney." His expression went sour for a second. "Some bloke is wondering what he's got, but knows it's worth a fortune. Good thing it was insured." Just as quickly, he flashed her a grin and faced her. "Come on, take pity on the poor foreigner." He brought her hand to his lips, kissing her knuckles. "Charlie and I do so want to ride a Ferris wheel."

Darcy hedged for a moment, glancing between him and Charlie. They looked like two puppies begging for a treat.

"I'm rather well off, and I love spending my money on beautiful women. Will that help sway you?"

"It would me," Meg said from the desk.

Oh for pity's sake. She knew when she was cornered, but misgivings haunted her. Kel was a fleeting kind of man, the kind who waltzed in and after some casual fun, waltzed right out. Nothing like Jack. That made her say, "If you promise to keep it light."

His smile couldn't have been more pleased. "Light as you like. Now, I'm off to get a car."

"A car?"

At the door, he looked back over his shoulder and said, "As much as I'd like that lovely body pressed up against me while on a motorcycle, I wouldn't want to endanger the boy."

"I have a car, Kel."

He reared back, looking offended. "Well that's just not-a-tall proper. See you later. Bye, Charles."

Smiling, he left the shop and hopped on the bike. Every woman in the salon let out a sigh as he drove away.

"My heavens, he's like a whirlwind," someone said, and Darcy thought it was Zoe. She couldn't be sure, her heart was pounding too hard to think clearly.

Oh, man. Oh, man, oh, man. What was she thinking?

Men asked questions, men wanted personal information, and she was letting a stranger near Charlie?

She'd have to be extra careful.

Kel seemed like a nice guy, but then so had Maurice at one time.

Chapter 8

The amusement park was wild with noise and the scent of hot dogs, popcorn and fried falafel. Music blasted over speakers, showering down on the people crowding the old stockyards. Teenagers walked hand in hand, parents corralled kids, and bells went off when someone won a prize.

Charlie was fascinated, and from his perch on Kel's shoulders, he had a bird's-eye view of everything. Darcy glanced up at her son. He was in kiddie heaven, his face smeared with cotton candy, his hands in Kel's hair. Kel didn't seem to mind and had a hold of Charlie's sneakered feet for balance.

She was grateful. Her son was heavy, and trying

to keep a hold of his hand in the crush of people had been murder on her nerves.

"When I was a boy we had a county fair," Kel was saying. "Nothing like this."

"You mean nothing expensive, loud and gaudy?"

The area was well-lit with strings of lights and every stand, ride or entertainment such as the house of mirrors had flashing lights and some roadie hawking for customers.

He smiled at her. "Yes. You're not having a good time?"

"As a matter-of-fact, I am." She popped a piece of sugary funnel cake in her mouth.

That smile grew bigger, showing perfect white teeth. He'd been polite, friendly, not touching her, and yet lavishing attention on Charlie. The way to a woman's heart is through her child? If it was, Jack beat him to the punch, she thought, then frowned at the thought. Had she been comparing the two men all evening?

Kel played with Charlie, accommodated him. Jack listened and talked at his level, as if everything her son said was important. Darcy didn't want Charlie to get attached to any man, to spare his feelings should they be forced to disappear again, but she also understood and accepted that her son had no man in his life to emulate, so he connected easily with Jack. And now, with Kel.

"I've been talking about myself all evening, Piper."

"And it's been interesting. Some of the things you've done to get a photo would be considered crazy."

"I'd rather think of it as doing the things I want, but with a camera in my hands." His gaze moved over her face. "I'd love to shoot you."

"No, thank you."

"Really? You're very pretty. Damn sexy I might add."

She tucked her hair behind her ear and gave him an embarrassed smile. "Thank you, but I don't photograph well and I'd rather it not be blatantly obvious to anyone else." The truth was, Darcy hadn't had her picture taken in years except for necessary IDs, and those were false. It was too dangerous to let a stranger who published his work in national magazines take photos of her.

When they arrived at the longed-for Ferris wheel, Charlie nearly toppled back as he leaned to look up.

Kel swung him down. "Are you sure, lad?"

Charlie nodded vigorously, hopping from foot to foot.

Kel looked at her, blandly. "I do believe he's rather excited."

"He leans toward you if he decides to replay the hot dogs and cotton candy you just fed him."

Kel laughed, offered the attendant the tickets, and in a minute or two they were riding high above the park.

Darcy thought she'd be sick as the seat swung back and forth. They dangled in a box a hundred feet above the crowd and Darcy felt her world tilt. Good God.

She was up here with her baby and a man she knew only by his name! The risks hit her hard, and like the string she was trying to cut with Maurice, once it was severed, what then? Would she fall into the life she wanted or be disappointed?

What changes would her life take? She looked down and her stomach rolled. She'd been alone for so long, on the edge of life, a fake one, and she desperately wanted a clean slate. So she could be who she really was without fear. What would that be like? To never worry. Heaven, she thought. Victory.

She glanced at her son. Charlie's eyes were as big as saucers, his attention shooting all over the park as he pointed out rides and vendors' stands. But when he started wiggling in the seat, both she and Kel put their arm across Charlie's front.

Darcy swore Kel won her over right then.

"Settle down, honey," she said as the ride took its last turn, thank God. And here she had worried about Charlie retching up the junk food?

"Can we go again? Please, please," Charlie begged, looking between the adults. Covertly, she rolled her eyes, hoping Kel noticed she was on the verge of losing her dinner.

"I'll tell you what, Charles," Kel said with English dignity. "We'll have us a bit of a snack, then take one more turn around the grounds."

"You mean we have to leave?" That pout was too cute to resist.

"It's nearly nine, lad," he said kindly, glancing briefly at Darcy. "But we can't leave before we try our hand at the duck hunt."

Charlie's face lit up at the prospect of firing a water pistol at plastic ducks. Kel hoisted Charlie up on his shoulders again.

Darcy whispered, "Thanks. But tell the truth, you just want to play."

"Oh, yes." He hurried off, Charlie bouncing like a rag doll, and Darcy kept up, not about to let her boy out of her sight. While Charlie was satisfied with a couple games, Kel wasn't, and dragged them all over the place, slapping down a dollar for the chance at a stuffed pink panther.

"One must have at least a gaudy reminder."

."I think you have more than your share." He'd won a cheap kids' backpack, which was stuffed with trinkets and toys.

"But Charlie likes them, right?" He looked down at the boy.

But Charlie was gone.

Darcy's heart slammed to a stop. Frantically, she looked around, then rushed into the crowd, panic slicing her as she dashed from spot to spot, calling his name. Kel went in the other direction, crouching low, and hollering for the boy.

Darcy's eyes burned, her terror scrambling her brain, images of Charlie kidnapped or hurt breaking down her common sense. She'd taught him well, she thought, to yell, to scream for help, but what if he couldn't, what if—she heard her name, and turned sharply. She expected Kel.

She got Jack.

With Charlie in his arms.

She ran, grabbing Charlie from him and hugging him tightly. "Oh baby, oh honey."

"I fell down, Mama. I'm sorry."

"I know, honey, I know." Thank God. Oh, thank God.

"He saw me and was running when someone knocked him over. I found him under a vendor's cart, trying not to get trampled," Jack said.

She forced back her tears, leaning to look at Charlie. She kissed his face, and Charlie caught hers between his tiny hands and said calmly, "Don't cry, Mama. I didn't get hurt."

Darcy choked on her relief. "I'm so glad, honey, but don't leave my side, ever, not for a second. Ever."

His lower lip curled down and Charlie glanced at Jack.

"Your mother's right, sport."

She hugged him again, looking over his shoulder at Jack and tearily whispered, "Thank you so much."

Jack moved closer, running his hand over Charlie's hair. "Are you here alone with him?"

"No, actually, she's with me." Kel stopped by her side, putting his arm around her and squeezing and looking deep into her eyes. "I can't imagine the panic you just felt, but I saw it." He had such a sad look just then, Darcy was taken aback.

Her gaze moved to Jack's. Oh, dear. If that glare was armed, it could kill. "Jack, this is Kel Adams."

Jack looked hard enough at Kel that he stepped away from her, lowered his arm. He didn't offer a handshake, either.

"I think we've had enough excitement for the day, wouldn't you say?" Kel said into the silence.

Darcy nodded. Kel went back for the bag of prizes, insisting it would just end the evening on a sour note without them.

Jack just stood there, staring after the man.

"That was rude, Jack."

His gaze snapped back to her. "Who is this guy?"

"A client, and a photographer."

"And?"

"And nothing, Jack. I just met him."

"And you're dating him? With Charlie?"

Why did that sound so bad? Was it because of all the times he'd asked her out and she'd refused? Yet she let him into her home, let him know things about her most people never did.

"It's just a night out, nothing more." She frowned harder. "You're jealous." It almost choked her.

He looked away, then back at her, not admitting a thing. Did she want him to? A little voice in her head said, yes, be jealous, be my champion, take some of these burdens. But she couldn't and knew she could handle them herself. She was just so tired of doing it all alone.

"What are you doing here?" she asked. "This isn't a place I'd expect you to be."

"It's not, without good reason." His gaze landed pointedly on Charlie, and he moved in, moved close. Darcy felt swept away by his nearness. There was so much strength there, she thought. So much quiet nobility. Didn't anyone else see it?

Then he said, "I volunteered to help the police keep order."

Darcy felt an instant of panic, then settled. Jack was tightly linked to the police. He hunted their bail jumpers for the court, but in the same instance that brought concern that he'd reveal something about her, she dismissed it. Jack didn't tell anyone anything about himself; he wouldn't betray her. Would he?

He must have noticed her alarm because he laid a hand on her arm. "What's wrong, Piper?"

"Nothing," she said, hugging her son.

His look went deeper. "There'll come a day when you'll have to trust me, and stop running from it."

Just then Kel walked up with the pack. Darcy barely glanced his way, then looked back at Jack. He was already melting into the crowd.

For a second, she wanted to go after him, but didn't know what she'd say. Or why. Why did the man always leave her so confused? Right now she would trade all her secrets to just share one honest moment with him.

Too dangerous, she thought, and she left with Kel.

Charlie was sound asleep in the back seat before they left the parking lot. They didn't say much as he drove toward her place. She'd considered having him drop her off at the shop where he'd picked them up, so he wouldn't know where she lived, but he could ask a couple questions and learn that too easily. Short of living in a cave in the hills, Darcy could only hide so deep.

Darcy glanced back at her son slumped in his car seat. His face was still sticky, his lips purple from the last snow cone. His head was squashing a cheap Velveteen rabbit. "I was so scared," she blurted. "He's everything to me."

He patted her hand. "I know, Piper, I know." After a moment he asked, "So do I have to get my hair cut so you'll go out with me again?"

"No. But a pedicure would hedge your bet," she said, trying to lighten her own mood.

He frowned. "Very unmanly. And I wouldn't want to spoil my image with the public display of my ugly feet."

Darcy was still laughing when they reached her house. Leaving Kel on the porch, she slipped inside to put Charlie in his bed. When she came out, Kel was standing in the foyer. She frowned at him, and he immediately stepped back out of the house to the porch.

"Nice place."

"Thank you." Darcy pulled the door closed behind her, leaning back against the frame. She wasn't inviting him in. It might be rude, but her house was her sanctuary from her business, her fears. Her thoughts jumped to Jack, the deadly look he'd given Kel, the questions.

The man was too hard to figure out.

"I had a nice time," she said.

"So did I. Maybe next time we can go out alone?"

"Gee, and here I thought it was Charlie you were dating tonight?"

He looked endearingly bashful just then. "Bit overexcited, was I?"

"It was cute."

"Ah, now I'm making points."

"You're keeping a score?"

"If one doesn't know the level he wishes to reach, then one can't strive to achieve it."

Darcy laughed. *Very Winston Churchill,* she thought. "And what is it that you wanted to achieve?"

"To get to know you." He moved closer, crowding her a little. "And to taste that mouth."

"You promised we'd keep it light, remember?"

"I promise." Still, he grinned.

Then he slid his arm around her waist and tugged her gently against his length as he tipped his head.

"Kel?"

"Yes?"

Darcy felt her insides go soft and liquid at the tender look in his eyes. "This is not light."

"No, this is just a kiss."

His mouth lay over hers, soft and molding. Noting aggressive, but simply an…introduction. It was gloriously patient and romantic. Nothing like the raw, consuming energy she'd shared just inches from Jack.

At the thought of the bounty hunter, Darcy broke the kiss and Kel stepped back as if it had been his choice, not hers.

He blew out a breath, looking her over. "'Night." He spun away, and trotted down the steps.

Darcy went inside and leaned back against the closed door, wondering what kind of woman she was if she could have thoughts of Jack Turner while she was kissing another man on the front porch.

She wasn't a hypocrite.

But right now, she felt as if she were betraying some part of herself.

By the next evening, her brain was fried and she was burning a candle at both ends and wishing she had two more to light. Between searching for information on Porche and something on surrogates, she was exhausted.

Radio ads she couldn't track; TV was pointless since surrogates were not the norm then. Her only option was print media. She was about to call it quits for the night when she pulled up a library archive of a newspaper in west Arizona, close enough to Athena Academy to alert her. The *Mesa Centennial*. Never heard of the paper, but that didn't mean much. She'd read twenty-year-old ads from every print media in three states. The ad read simply. *Surrogate mother wanted. 50K, expenses paid. Must sign contract.* There was a number and she tried it. No such listing, a recording said.

The name reference to the ad was not listed.

Probably paid for in cash and mailed. Anonymous.

She decided to place her own in several newspapers in the surrounding area, asking for information on surrogates. Hers read just as simply, specifying dates, yet offered a money reward up-front. She'd know what to ask if anyone answered just to make a buck off it.

That done, she sent an e-mail to the Cassandras, giving them a progress report, then focused on Porche.

By now, Darcy knew the woman's statistics inside out. She'd even found a copy of her yearbook, which had her signature, Patty Fogerty, scanned under her picture.

Darcy needed an expert to compare all the signatures that were signed at different times, and when she mention it to Megan, her pal said she took a yoga class with a woman who analyzed handwriting. At first Darcy had thought it was like palm reading till Megan insisted her friend worked for the police department.

Which made her very credible.

Megan had begged a favor from Loni Marks and Darcy would meet with the woman as soon as she had more tangible evidence for her to do a comparison. Darcy needed to compare the past and most recent signatures. The dates were what really mattered to Darcy. Porche Fairchild had signed a document authorizing the loan of funding for a production. That's what she had found in Maurice's office. Although the film had gone into production three weeks after Porche was last seen, her signature had been required before that, when the money was transferred. The day *after* Maurice had come home hugging his briefcase. The signatures should all match, and Darcy was relying a lot on a hunch that they wouldn't.

If they did match, then she was out of luck. It meant Porche had been alive when the documents were signed. Though Darcy didn't want anyone to be dead, non-matching signatures would tell her that Maurice forged the papers. That would turn suspicion on someone at the bank where the draft was issued. Thirty-five million was a big chunk of change to let go without a lot of verification. Who had Maurice forced to do that, and how?

She tried again to reach Porche's assistant, and after persistent calls she finally got Marianna Vasquez on the line.

Darcy introduced herself as she had on the message she'd left, as a reporter doing a story for *Money Market* magazine about Ms. Fairchild and her sudden and now longtime absence from the financial world.

"Why now? She's been gone three years. It is because she was mentioned on the news last week?"

"Partly. It's a follow-up. We did do a story three months after she left for Europe, but no one in the England, France or Germany offices had seen or heard from her."

"I don't know what I can tell you. Ms Fairchild just…left the country. I mean, she didn't even come into the office, only left a note and final instructions for closing up."

"And the note said?"

"Aside from the instructions about turning off the utilities, it said that she was leaving, that the last loan was complete and that Maurice Steele had everything he needed to finalize the production money from the bank. All Porche had to do was sign the final draft. And she did."

Darcy's heart dropped with her spirits. "You're certain of it?"

"Well I'm looking at it now. When you left a message last time, I brought the file to the office."

"Can you fax it to me?" Darcy switched on the fax and gave her the number. "What was her behavior before she left?" she asked when she came back on the line.

"Agitated and angry. She didn't get mad often, but someone was upsetting her."

"Do you have any idea who?"

"No. She was working five deals at once. Always was. But that wasn't unusual. She was a workaholic."

That played against Porche's closing up shop and heading to Europe, Darcy thought. Had Maurice paid the loan back, and if so, how? Where was Porche's share going? Tax wise, he had to put it somewhere. Probably into an account he never touched to cover his tracks.

"My magazine's theory is that she didn't leave on her own power."

Marianna's voice lowered. "What are you saying?"

"Foul play."

Marianna's pitch rose with her excitement. "See, the police didn't investigate very much because she left that note saying she was leaving for Europe and put her entire business on hold. I wasn't happy about it because I've got a kid and needed my job."

"What did you do?"

"I told the police that she wouldn't have left like that. She lived for her work. The woman loved numbers more than anyone I know."

"But my records show they didn't file a report."

"No, they didn't." Her tone slid into bitterness. "They accepted the note, and did investigate, but since her house was already listed for sale with a real-estate broker, plus her household goods and car were in storage, they figured she was doing just as she said. The police said she got on a private jet for Europe."

Could Porche have already decided to take a long vacation, or move, and the timing had been just right?

Damn. This was not looking good. "But did she get off the jet?"

"I don't know. I guess they confirmed that. Wouldn't they?"

"Yes, they would. But if all evidence points to her

wanting some time alone, then why pursue further?" People were allowed to disappear.

"Because this is just not like her."

"I'm inclined to believe that odd behavior for someone who was so analytical is cause for question," Darcy said.

"Yeah, ditto."

Darcy glanced at her notes. "Had she mentioned closing her business to you before?"

"No, she hadn't. That's what struck me as so strange."

"Where did she go the night before she left?"

"She didn't say, but there was that deal with Steele."

"What did she think of Maurice Steele?"

Marianna's voice lowered. "She didn't care for him. She dealt with him because he paid through the nose in finance fees. See, the film had to show a profit on the first day, because that was where her cut came from. Pay the talent and the actual making of the film with the loan, and from the box-office sales, pay the finance charge, which was Porche's money, then the loan and get your share. So the pressure was on him. The rates would jump if the box-office sales didn't bring in enough to pay out early."

"Sounds like loan sharking."

"Yeah, doesn't it?" Marianna snickered. "But it's all legal. Steele cofinanced half himself, so that put him in deeper. Film companies only want the money for a year or so, for filming and production, till the release date. So short-term, high-interest loans are best. By reputation, Steele's films pay off in the first few weeks. But the last couple had pulled only a few million, which in this day is a bomb. The lead actor wasn't the public's version of an action star, either. So, for the rest of the money, I'd say half, Steele had to come to Porche. Getting the money was his job."

Darcy knew that. Maurice had used his stellar reputation to back films that were destined for late-night television, and she remembered him losing money on a couple and how agitated it had made him.

The fax finally printed and Darcy snatched it up. "Tell me one thing. Has Miss Fairchild contacted you at all in the last three years?"

"No. But she paid me my last month's pay and a decent severance bonus. I guess she forgot about the deal we'd made that if she went out of business, I'd be the first she'd sell it to."

"She didn't offer?"

"No, not that I could have afforded to buy her out, anyway."

"Miss Vasquez, could you fax me some information, some of her papers?"

"I don't know...."

"I think you might be on to something about her disappearance." *Make her feel like the hero,* Darcy thought. *Because she just might be.* "I can't find anyone who has laid eyes on her—and I've got great resources."

"Listen, Ms. Daniels. I liked Porche, she was bright, and sharp and she had a great sense of humor. She was good to me, very good. I'd like to see her again, and if what you're saying is true, that means someone hurt her."

"Yes, that's a very viable possibility."

There was a stretch of silence, then, "Thank God someone thinks so." Darcy heard the long, tired breath through the phone. "No one believed me, and just because she worked in the Hollywood crowd, they cast her sudden disappearance off as movie weirdness. Not me. This woman spent Christmas with me and my little girl." Her voice fractured and Darcy realized that Marianna loved Porche. "We were close."

How close she wasn't going to get into now.

"I'm going to send you that last file by fax," Marianna said. "You can call me later. Since the police didn't suspect foul play, I have a lot of her papers. But I really have to get off the phone and go back to work. This boss isn't nearly as sympathetic as Porche was."

"Thank you, I understand. And, Ms. Vasquez?"

"Yes?"

"Keep this to yourself. We don't want to tip our hand to anyone."

"You got it."

Darcy hung up, relaxing back in the chair as the fax spit out pages of old contracts. It would take her a couple days to go through them. But she would.

How exactly she was going to present this to the authorities without putting herself in danger or losing Charlie was still a mystery. A parental kidnapper didn't have much clout.

She rubbed her face, her mind crowded with too many thoughts and concerns. Her unlisted cell phone rang and she looked around, trying to remember where she'd left it. She made a dive for her purse and hit send.

The voice on the other end was low and scratchy, as if too much drinking and smoking had worn out the vocal cords. Yet when the man spoke, Darcy's heart dropped.

"You the one looking for stuff on a surrogate?"

Chapter 9

This has to be the sleaziest place in town, Darcy thought, stepping into the Match Lite Bar on the edge of Phoenix, Arizona. Far outside the edge. And from the looks of the clientele, the local gene pool needed a filter. Or at least some bleach.

Dressed in faded, worn, low-riding jeans and a red top that revealed just enough flesh to distract, Darcy popped gum in her mouth and walked deeper into the dimly lit bar. The bartender spotted her and, leaving the customer he was chatting with, he moved down toward her.

He was bald, beefy, looked sorta like Mr. Clean, and had forgotten to use a razor this morning. He gave her the once-over, a little grin showing his approval, and she returned the stare.

"What'll you have, sweet thing?"

"Bourbon, neat."

That seemed to please him and when he brought it back, she leaned over, showing enough breast to keep him interested, and said, "I'm looking for Tony Feeley."

"Touchy?"

Touchy Feeley? Good God. That was a name? "Yeah." Tony Feeley was supposed to meet her outside the Match Lite. When he hadn't shown, the roughnecks on the street forced her inside.

"You one of his girls?"

She frowned, sipping the liquor. "I have better taste than that."

"Then what's a pretty little thing like you want with that pimp?"

Great, she thought, keeping her features impassive. The man that had answered her ad for information on surrogates, saying all the right things, pandered women. Her fingers tightened on the glass.

"He's got my sister's kid, and I aim to get her back."

He scoffed rudely. "Fat chance, honey."

Leaning forward on the bar, her forearms braced, she said, "You'd be surprised what I can do, handsome." She popped her gum, looking him over as if he was double-chocolate cake. "Describe him for me, will you, baby? I wanna see him before he sees me."

The bartender's eyes narrowed. "You a cop?"

She hopped back, opening her jacket, showing the knife sheathed at her hip and the fake navel ring. Instead of a wig, she'd put a red henna rinse on her hair and clipped it up at odd angles in tiny girly barrettes. "Do I look like cop material?"

He was practically licking his lips. "You look like dessert."

She leaned over the scarred wood bar again, her voice low and breathy. "But we ain't had dinner yet."

He grinned, glancing around to make certain no one was within earshot. "He's skinny, black hair, goatee, squirrelly little eyes. Wears a long brown leather coat, pointed-toe boots. He kicks with them."

"Like a girl?"

The bartender snickered. "Yeah." He inclined his head toward a side door. "Most days you can find him in the alley."

"Real entrepreneur, huh?"

"Just be careful."

She was kind of touched that the hard-ball bartender would even care. "Thanks, honey," she said, then tossed back the bourbon, paid, and left through the front door.

Outside, she glanced around. There were a lot of

derelicts and foot traffic. For two blocks the streets were lit with neon signs advertising booze, lap dancing and sex shows. Cars cruised, hydraulic shocks bouncing them down the street. The curbs reeked of urine and vomit.

Darcy wished she had a gun. She didn't want to get close enough to anyone to use her knife. Walking toward the alley, she stopped at the edge. A single lightbulb shone down on the filth, lighting the huge trash container outside the bar's side door. Opposite that, there were side entrances to the neighboring building, a couple drunks lounging on the thresholds and teens making deals or just smoking weed. They didn't spare her a glance.

Darcy said a quick prayer, pulled her jacket to conceal her knife and started walking, wanting to hold her nose. Instead, she breathed through her mouth. It wasn't much better.

"You looking for Touchy?" came in slurred words.

She spun, knife out. The drunk in the doorway snickered and tipped his bottle to his lips, unmoved.

"Where is he?"

He gave her a one-eyed stare. "He just took off with someone. Well…they was draggin' him off." The drunk gestured with the bottle and Darcy moved fast, rounding the edge of the building. There were a couple warehouses a block away, an abandoned building separated by a parking lot with junk cars

GET FREE BOOKS and a FREE GIFT WHEN YOU PLAY THE...

Lucky 7

SLOT MACHINE GAME!

Just scratch off the silver box with a coin. Then check below to see the gifts you get!

YES!

I have scratched off the silver box. Please send me the 2 free Silhouette Bombshell® books and gift for which I qualify. I understand I am under no obligation to purchase any books, as explained on the back of this card.

300 SDL D34A   **200 SDL D34C**

FIRST NAME	LAST NAME

ADDRESS

APT.#	CITY

STATE/PROV.	ZIP/POSTAL CODE

7	7	7	**Worth TWO FREE BOOKS** plus a **BONUS Mystery Gift!**
🍒	🍒	🍒	**Worth TWO FREE BOOKS!**
♣	♣	♣	**Worth ONE FREE BOOK!**
🔔	🔔	🍒	**TRY AGAIN!**

www.eHarlequin.com

(S-B-08/04)

DETACH AND MAIL CARD TODAY!

The Silhouette Reader Service™ — Here's how it works:

Accepting your 2 free books and gift places you under no obligation to buy anything. You may keep the books and gift and return the shipping statement marked "cancel." If you do not cancel, about a month later we'll send you 4 additional books and bill you just $4.69 each in the U.S., or $5.24 each in Canada, plus 25¢ shipping & handling per book and applicable taxes if any.* That's the complete price and — compared to cover prices of $5.50 each in the U.S. and $6.50 each in Canada — it's quite a bargain! You may cancel at any time, but if you choose to continue, every month we'll send you 4 more books, which you may either purchase at the discount price or return to us and cancel your subscription.
*Terms and prices subject to change without notice. Sales tax applicable in N.Y. Canadian residents will be charged applicable provincial taxes and GST. Credit or debit balances in a customer's account(s) may be offset by any other outstanding balance owed by or to the customer.

If offer card is missing write to: Silhouette Reader Service, 3010 Walden Ave., P.O. Box 1867, Buffalo NY 14240-1867

BUSINESS REPLY MAIL
FIRST-CLASS MAIL   PERMIT NO. 717-003   BUFFALO, NY

POSTAGE WILL BE PAID BY ADDRESSEE

SILHOUETTE READER SERVICE
3010 WALDEN AVE
PO BOX 1867
BUFFALO NY 14240-9952

NO POSTAGE
NECESSARY
IF MAILED
IN THE
UNITED STATES

and a group of people hovering around the flames in a barrel. More than half were passed out on the ground under cut-open cardboard boxes.

She scanned the area and in the distance, saw a man being thrown back against a black car. He fit the bartender's description. A big blonde delivered a crushing blow to the man's middle, then backhanded him before pressing a gun to his forehead.

Oh hell.

Even from this far, she knew it had to be Feeley.

Darcy bolted, running hard.

Feeley was her only lead, and leaving him to be worked over by two men in dark biker clothes wasn't in her plans. Fake bikers, she thought, running. The neat haircuts were a dead giveaway. Money, polished—hired muscle.

She headed right for them, and when they heard her, the men turned.

Feeley looked at her as if he'd seen a ghost.

Darcy stopped short. The men ogled her with open sexual interest, easing their grip.

"Help me," Feeley said.

"Shut up, asshole," one man, a Latino, said, holding Feeley against the car. The other man, the blonde, turned the gun on her. "Get outta here."

Darcy stilled, fear jolting up her spine as she circled, making them follow her, making them turn from Feeley.

"I just want to talk to him for a second, guys," she said. "Nothing big."

"This ain't your business. Get outta here, bitch."

She gave them her best affronted look. "You talk to your mama with that mouth?"

"Shut up." The Latino inclined his head to the other. His blond partner headed toward her.

"Stay out of this, lady," Blondie said.

"Probably good advice."

Blondie moved toward her, smiling. Not seeing her as a threat. When he got close, Darcy executed a high double kick that connected with his jaw, the first snapping his head back, the second dropping blond babe to the ground. Latino guy pointed the weapon at her and fired. But he was way off target because Feeley struggled and Darcy was already diving for the ground, out of the path, rolling and coming up close enough to knock the gun aside, spin, then slam her elbow into his face. He howled, falling back and shaking his head.

Blood shot out like sputters from a dying sprinkler. Feeley took off as she plowed her fist into the guy's solar plexus, knocking the wind out of him. The jolt rang up her arm. Oh, that hurt. The guy's wearing a Kevlar vest. Jeez.

Darcy stepped back as Blondie struggled for air, pushing himself up. Feeley was moving fast down the alley and she let out an irritated sigh, kicked the gun into the high grass, then glanced around for something to do some damage. Rushing to the right, she grabbed a rusted pipe off the ground. When the blonde tried to get to his feet, Darcy brought it down on the back of his head. Hard. He dropped, motionless.

Latino came after her, bloody and pissed.

But Darcy was just as ticked off. Three years' worth of anger and frustration came out when he lunged for her. She swiped the pipe like a sword, smacking his arm. The bone cracked. Latino dropped to his knees, howling and holding his arm. Darcy swung again, knocking him in the head, and he went over like a sinking ship. Alive, but out for now. She threw down the pipe, then chased after Feeley.

The little weasel wasn't getting away. As far as she was concerned, Tony "Touchy" Feeley owed her his life. She pushed herself hard, that shot of liquor magnifying her determination to reach Tony before he disappeared into a town she didn't know.

She knocked over a crate, leaped a discarded bumper and gained on him. His long coat was stylin', but the impractical boots were slowing him down. He glanced back and Darcy was on him, diving for his back and knocking him to the ground. He scrambled to get up and she latched on to his boot, and pulled out her knife.

"Move and I cut the pretty-boy boots."

He snapped a look at her, small eyes narrowing. "Get off, bitch." He kicked out. Darcy ducked and put the blade's edge to the boots.

"I can just as easily give you back to the men in black."

His eyes flared and Darcy felt triumph coming. Keeping a hold of his boot, she crouched to her knees. "What'd they want, Feeley, bad debt, territory?"

"They were going to kill me."

"Why?"

"To keep me from talking to *you*."

It was Darcy's turn to look stunned. They must have seen the ad. How did they know she was coming? She'd covered her tracks, driving the few hours from Comanche. She shoved off and stood, replacing her knife and waiting till Feeley got to his feet. Then she slammed him against the alley wall.

"It's not nice to make a deal, then renege on it, Feeley. Bad for the pimp reputation, you know?"

"Are you nuts, lady? They were going to kill me!"

"You said that. So considering you're still breathing, you owe me, huh?"

"I ain't saying nothin'."

When he moved, no doubt to get a weapon, Darcy braced her arm against his throat, cutting off his air supply and searching him. She found a stiletto in a slim pocket inside his coat. She kept it, patting him down for more and found brass knuckles and a black-jack. Tough-guy equipment, and she could only imagine how often he used them on women. She pocketed them all.

"What? No gun?"

"They took it."

Darcy glanced to the right, checking to see if Biker Boys had roused enough to hunt her. She had to hurry. "You answered the ad, Touchy. Talk. Why didn't those men want you to talk to me?"

"Hell if I know! You gonna give me some air?"

She pushed harder. "Tell me what you know!"

"Why should I?" He shifted his leg to kick and Darcy whipped out her knife, pressing the point to his groin.

"Because, Mr. Feeley, if you don't, the men in black will have no reason to kill you. Tell and they can come after me."

Darcy wasn't letting that happen. This wasn't like the rescues with Jack. She didn't have a safety net and had risked her life too much tonight already. She was damn lucky she'd gotten the jump on those guys, and she wasn't pressing it further.

"You're just a chick."

"At the moment that hardly matters, does it? Tell me why you answered my ad."

His eyes narrowed. "I saw it and remembered I

had a girl a long time ago. She was into some surrogate deal. You don't forget someone who'd have a
baby for strangers, you dig? They were gonna pay
her fifty grand to push out a kid. She promised to
give me a cut for her time off."

The woman must have been desperate, she
thought. "She tricked for you."

"Yeah. She wanted out, but owed me for her crib,
essentials and the time off. Nine months." He smirked.

"She was willing to have a baby to pay you off?
Sounds like an honorable woman."

"She was a fucking whore."

"And that makes you what, Touchy?"

His nose actually tipped the air. "Her man, her
protection. Her keeper. She owed me!"

This guy was unbelievable, and as far as Darcy
was concerned, he was no better than an abusive
husband. A slave trader. And she wasn't ready to believe everything he said. But then at this point, why
lie? "Did she have the baby?"

"Hell if I know."

"Didn't you collect her debt to you?"

"She split. I didn't need the money that bad."

She shoved him into the threshold of a side door.
"You're lying. Someone tell you to leave her alone?"

Feeley just stared back, unmoved.

"What did you tell those guys?" She inclined her
head in their general direction.

"Nothin'. They seemed to know what I knew already."

Great, Darcy thought, she had a trail. "Where's this woman now?"

"Christ, you want me to draw you a map?" She put pressure on his windpipe. "Last I heard she was in Vegas, dancing or something." He cleared his throat. "Always was a better dancer than she was a whore."

Darcy stared, wondering what made people like this. "Your level of humanity is remarkable."

"Yeah, yeah. Blow me."

Darcy released him. He shook his jacket into place, smoothed his oily black hair and gave her a smirk.

He stepped toward her, maliciousness in his ugly face, and she moved in his path. "Don't try it." She caught her knife by the tip and eyed his boots. "I won't be so kind."

"I told you what you wanted. What the fuck else do you want?"

"A name."

"Forget it."

"Why do you care?"

He eyed her and the nine-inch knife. "Because you'll kill me then."

"I saved your life, idiot. I should have let them have you," she said, disgusted.

"You need me." He smirked.

She glanced down the alley in both directions, then looked back at Touchy. He was backing toward the shadows. "Not anymore." She started walking.

"Hey, gimme my goods."

"Drop dead." Darcy didn't break stride.

"Her name is Cleo," he finally said.

Darcy stopped, casting a look back over her shoulder. "Say again?"

"Cleo Patra."

She frowned. "That can't be real."

His gaze shot nervously to the ends of the alley and he took a couple steps. "No, it's a stage name, no one uses real names down here. Change your name, hide your past, you dig?"

Darcy knew that probably better than this Cleo woman. "Except you. Anthony Degas Feeley, from Reno." His small eyes rounded. "The Vegas police have a warrant out for you, you know."

He sneered. "So what else is new? Gimme my stuff."

Darcy kept the stiletto, but held out the other junk. It would have tipped a boat, it was so heavy. He moved toward her and she pulled it back. "Describe her."

"Tall, big tits. African. She was twenty-five or so when she split."

Darcy dropped the gear and hurried to the entrance of the alley.

"Hey what about my reward?"

"You have your life, Touchy. I'd say we're even."

"Bitch."

"That's queen bitch." She faced him. He was gathering up his piles of metal. She pitched the roll of bills at him and he snatched it up like a hungry dog.

"Steer me wrong, Touchy, and I'll send the cops after you."

"Lady, are you stupid? The cops ain't got shit on those guys. You're stepping into some dangerous shit. If you wanna die, keep looking for Cleo." He darted into the shadows and for a breath, Darcy watched him slither along the side of the building, then disappear. A real rat.

Not wanting to encounter the men in black again, she left the alley and moved down the street, weaving between people and checking behind herself for the hired creeps. Her heart pounded like a hammer, her senses alert for anyone moving toward her, but prostitutes and drunks shifted past as if she didn't exist.

It took her a half hour to get far enough away that she could hail a cab, and when she did, she gave the guy an extra ten to make a couple turns around the block before heading toward her hotel.

On the first pass, she spotted the goons in black just coming out of the Match Lite, looking bloody and pissed, and she scrunched down in the seat for a couple blocks. Then on the second pass, she eased up, looking behind.

"Driver, slow down and pull over." As he did, Darcy hunched on the seat, looking out the rear window. The goons were gone. Yet before she faced front, a man stepped under the single bulb that lit the front door of the bar. Her heart slammed to her stomach. Jack? He was paying a man, or handing him something. When he looked up to scan the street, Darcy was certain it was him.

Black hat, bomber jacket, long legs. Yeah, that was him.

She sank into the seat, ignoring the cab driver's curious glances in the rearview mirror. "Drive on, please. And thank you."

Just because Jack was here didn't mean that he was tailing her. He was a bounty hunter. He was always after a jumper.

Her thoughts shifted to her one solid lead.

Cleo Patra.

In Las Vegas. Sin city. She couldn't take Charlie with her. It wasn't a place for a child by any means, and she wasn't putting her son in danger for anything. Those men were willing to kill Touchy to keep him from talking to anyone, and since she'd been meeting Touchy to find out about a woman who'd become a surrogate twenty years ago, the weak link was suddenly a viable connection to the egg mining.

And more dangerous than any of the Cassandras expected.

They'd found Touchy after she'd placed the ad and spoken to him. Had they bugged his phone? Seen the ad? Been watching all this time? It was pretty obvious that they understood the ad enough to go after Touchy. He was a link to this Cleo woman.

Darcy was part of that chain now, and though no one knew her name, the number in the paper was her "rescue" cell number. Although it was unlisted, with some smart computer hacking, it could be traced.

This was a little more danger than she'd bargained for. Way more.

But she had to go to Vegas, and the safest place for Charlie was away from it all.

When Darcy arrived at home she was still scared, still looking over her shoulder for the boys in black. She did a complete check of her house, locking windows, and had her cell number changed. It didn't feel like enough, and she wondered when she wouldn't have to behave like a fleeing convict all the time. She sent another e-mail to the Cassandras, telling them the little she'd learned and that the source, Touchy Feeley, was not reliable. She'd have to find Cleo Patra to prove it and would go looking in a couple days. She also warned them about the danger that was nearly on her doorstep and was possibly coming to theirs.

She was tempted to confess her past right then, but the roadblocks weren't cleared away yet. She was still a parental kidnapper and involving them directly would expose them to aiding and abetting charges. She couldn't do that to them. Kayla, who knew the most, probably could guess how she was feeling. But she wasn't ready to talk openly about it with the Cassandras, no matter how much she wanted their support right now.

Besides, all her theories about Maurice were just that, theories. She was hoping that document expert Loni Marks would shine some favorable light on the papers she'd taken from Maurice's safe. If she didn't, Darcy was really going to need the Cassandras' help. Because if Jack had seen her and Charlie on TV, there was a chance that Maurice might have, too. Her son would need more protection than just herself, and although Maurice wouldn't know Charlie by sight—he'd been an infant when she left—Athena Academy and Rainy's name might clue him in.

After a long workday, Darcy sat in Loni Marks's lab in the basement of her home, sipping vanilla coffee as Loni examined the papers. For Loni to confirm anything, she'd needed the original documents, and Marianna Vasquez had agreed without hesitation. Darcy had given her a post-office box to mail the papers to, and Marianna hadn't questioned its location. Darcy had, after all, portrayed herself as a freelance writer.

As Darcy watched Loni work, she was fascinated by the woman's methods. Not only was she a handwriting expert who could detect forgeries with ease, she was equipped to test ink and paper and could tell how many people had handled the paper and if different pens were used. Darcy was more than impressed.

Loni was certified by the American Board of Forensic Document Examiners and had worked for the U.S. Treasury Department, Secret Service for ten years, spotting bogus currency. Retired and at the disposal of police departments from Comanche to Las Vegas, Loni was called in on anything from counterfeit and forged documents to ones charred beyond recognition.

She must be more than just a yoga partner, Darcy thought, smiling. Loni was doing this on her own time as a favor to Megan.

Darcy was grateful for the help and had offered to pay her. Loni told her to put away her money, and reminded her that the private sector could rarely afford her services. Darcy accepted the kindness and shut up.

Right now, Loni was hunched over a microscope. Darcy estimated her age at around fifty, only because her hair was pure silver, a contrast to her face, barely wrinkled around the eyes, her complexion smooth. Documents of her achievements lined the walls, and while she dressed very hip, she had a no-nonsense, business-first manner that marked her as a highly sought-after professional.

And she made great coffee.

Around Loni on several different tables were workstations with tubes, chemicals and equipment Darcy wasn't going to try to understand.

"Tell me what you want to know, Piper."

"I need to know if that signature is real. Compared to the older ones, it looks the same to me."

"And the canceled bank draft?"

That was the draft Porche had given Maurice at the time she'd disappeared. Marianna had sent it, and Darcy needed to know if Fairchild had really signed it. "Well I'm not certain, but I think it's fake, too."

"Can I ask your interest in this?" Loni looked up, her gray-blue eyes penetrating.

"I'd rather not say right now. It's a hunch, and I don't want attention if it's nothing."

"Understandable." She went back to the pages under the microscope. She made notes, not saying a word, then went to another table, putting the paper under what looked like a copier. Darcy guessed that it wasn't.

"This paper is at least five years old, and I have five different sets of fingerprints."

"Can you find out whose?"

"Not here, but I can make a transfer of each set, if that would help."

Darcy didn't know how it would. Maurice, as far as she knew, had no prints on file. Perhaps Porche might have, since she was handling large amounts of money. But getting a comparison would be impossible since Darcy didn't want to get that close to the police.

"That would be good." She'd at least have them.

Loni put the paper through another set of tests, and machines spit out analyses, one after another. It took a while, and she admired the woman's patience.

Finally Loni returned to her desk, and Darcy poured her fresh coffee as she sat close.

"This is a real document, and this signature is authentic." She tapped Maurice's and had compared it to an old note Darcy had found in her date book. Five years ago, it had arrived with flowers, a diamond bracelet encircling one of the roses. It had been an apology from Maurice for speaking rudely to her, and at the time, Darcy had still had hope for their marriage.

She'd sold the bracelet for the down payment on her house.

"What about the other signature, Ms. Fairchild's?"

Loni looked over the rim of her half glasses and Darcy held her breath. "It's real."

Her shoulders sank.

"However…" Loni slid the bank draft for nearly twenty million across the desk. "This one is not."

Darcy stared at the draft, her heart pinging inside her chest. She lifted her gaze to Loni's, took a breath, then swallowed. "And the ones for the storage units, the business closures?"

"Forgeries. Good ones, done by an expert, I imagine, but forgeries."

Darcy sank into the chair, not smiling, her mind ticking off her next steps.

Then Loni said, "This is grand larceny, bank fraud, fraudulent identification, fraudulent commercial securities and electronic-funds transfer fraud. Aside from the forgery of a legal document, and I can think of about two other charges to add."

Darcy's gaze shifted to hers. "Good. But it's murder I'm trying to prove."

Loni's eyebrows shot up. "You need to give this to the police and the FBI."

"Oh, believe me, when I have enough, I will."

"You have enough now, Piper."

Darcy shook her head. "This person has money and power, Loni. He could buy his way out of this."

Loni tipped her head, her silver hair gleaming in the soft light. "You don't have much faith in the justice system, do you?"

Darcy stared back, indecision clawing at her dignity. "No, I don't. I was an abused wife, Loni, and I begged for help, from the police, from family and people who I'd thought were my friends.

But no one would help me. The cops wouldn't even come to the house when I called because my husband had more influence and if he didn't, he had close ties to those who did. He's a somebody, I'm a nobody."

Loni removed her specs, and picked up her coffee. "I can sympathize. I've seen it happen. It's a crime to ignore the call for help."

"This man—" she pointed to the papers, unwilling to reveal that it was her husband's signature Loni had been examining "—is the same. A power broker. Someone who thinks he can get away with anything because he's got money and prestige."

"Well, then, I will tell you another piece of information."

Darcy waited, almost breathless.

"This bank draft was signed by Maurice Steele. However, he was nervous when he signed it."

"Nervous?"

Loni inclined her head, and they stood and moved to the copierlike thing. Loni switched on the light and motioned for Darcy to have a look. "See the jerky edges of the *T* and *L?* That tells me he signed it but his hand was shaking. Now if it's from illness—"

"He's as fit as a twenty-year-old."

"Then he was nervous. And the same hesitation is found here and here." She pointed to Porche Fairchild's signature.

"Did he write it?"

"That was the other thing I was going to tell you. Yes, he did. The witness signature I can't be certain of without anything to compare, but I would go so far as to say yes, he signed that, too. The similarities are just too close. And this is my specialty, by the way."

"Would you document all this for me?"

Loni hesitated.

"This could lead to murder charges, Loni," Darcy pleaded. "Porche Fairchild was missing before that check was signed."

"How long?"

"At least a week."

"Have they found her?"

"No, and no one is looking. Except me." Darcy waited.

Loni finally nodded, and Darcy thought her knees would give out, she was so relieved.

"All right. I will."

"Thank you."

"But you have to promise me one thing," Loni said before Darcy could work up real excitement. "That you'll turn all this over to the police and won't go after this man yourself."

"I have no intention of confronting him."

"Good. Because with a jail threat like this coming, he could quite possibly try to kill you to keep you quiet."

"Of that I have no doubt."

The only thing Darcy had on her side right now was time, and that Maurice didn't know where she was.

Chapter 10

Darcy had one more appointment when Kel showed up, looking so fine in brown leather slacks and a long, butternut-colored jacket. As slick as you please he walked up and kissed her lightly.

Though she'd kissed him once before, she felt he was being awfully presumptuous.

"Where have you been, love?"

In the storeroom, Darcy kept putting away the new stock of tints. "I had some business to take care of, nothing big," she said, checking her invoice. "What have you been doing?"

"Oh, taking pictures, eating hot salsa and wanting to see you. You are about the busiest woman I've ever met."

"Know a lot of slackers, do you?"

He smiled, inching closer. "Can I talk you out of work for a bit?"

She made a little sound, half want, half denial. "I have customers."

Regardless, he slid his warm arm around her waist, not caring about the clipboard and pen, and dipped his head to kiss her more thoroughly. The clipboard sagged in her grip as his hands slid up her back.

The man knew how to kiss. A movie kiss.

Yet Darcy pushed him back. "Someone will see."

He grinned. "And this matters?"

"Charlie does, and this is my business."

He stepped back, rubbing his mouth and looking chagrined. "Yeah, I guess you're right. You shouldn't be so irresistible then."

How was she supposed get ticked at that?

"I had a bit of a chat with Charles."

It was cute that he called her son by his given name. "What about?"

"Oh, the usual guy stuff, worms living even after you cut them in half, motorcycles and that you're headed to Vegas."

She hesitated in putting away a box, then finished, wishing Charlie hadn't taken to Kel quite so readily. "Yes, I am. Just a quick trip." She hoped.

"And you're taking Charles? Seems like the last place you'd take a child."

She wasn't taking her son, but before she could answer, Meg knocked. She was grinning when she peered around the door. "Your next appointment is here."

There was something about the way she said it that put Darcy on alert.

"I'm ready." She set the clipboard down and she and Kel left the storeroom. Kel kissed her, spoke to Charlie, who was playing in the little pop-up tent Kel had bought him, then went to the door.

Darcy stopped short when she saw Jack Turner standing close. By the look on his face, he'd seen Kel kiss her.

Great.

Kel stopped in front of Jack and the two men stared. Jack had a "bull in the pen" look, and Darcy waited for one of them to paw the ground and charge. Kel glanced her way, winked, then left.

Jack came to her, stopping within inches, his gaze hard and piercing, though his voice was low. "You kiss all your male clients?"

"No, just the really good-looking ones."

His look said he didn't know whether to be pissed or pleased.

She put her hands on her hips. "Are you here for a trim or did you come in just to interrogate me in front of everyone?"

Jack let out a long breath, scraping his hand over his shaggy hair. He glanced at the clients, who were all too interested in their conversation. "No, I didn't. I'm sorry."

"Come on," she said, nodding to the shampoo center.

As she washed his hair, he kept his eyes closed, his hands to himself, not saying a word. When she was done, Charlie realized Jack was there and shrieked his name so loud they both winced. Jack tossed her the towel and bent, his arms open to catch the flying toddler diving for his knees.

Charlie wrapped his arms around Jack's neck and Jack looked almost honored. "How you doing, sport?"

Charlie gave him a big smile. "Great. I got a tent." He twisted to point.

"You do?" He glanced at Piper, then with Charlie in his arms, walked over to inspect the tent. Squatting, Jack gave it a good shake. "Seems solid. You having fun in there?"

Jack set Charlie down and the boy dived inside, where he had comic books he couldn't read yet, a blanket and a pillow. "You're all set for a night in the desert, huh?"

"Yeah, cool huh? Kel says I can go with him next time he goes to shoot pictures."

"Is that so?" Jack twisted to look at her. Darcy could tell his back teeth were grinding.

"Yeah. I have new crayons and why do they call blue cyan?"

Jack looked back at her son. "To be different, I guess."

Charlie asked about another half dozen questions at light speed, then finally took a breath to say, "Wanna see my books?"

"Sure, can I borrow one? I'll read while your mom's cutting my hair." Charlie held one up to him, proud to share his Spider-Man collection. Jack took it, flipping through it and telling Charlie, "This is great. I haven't read this issue."

Charlie beamed, and Jack slipped a tiny penlight from his back pocket, one with a plastic charm on the end, and handed it to Charlie. "This might come in handy in there."

"Wow," Charlie said, and Jack ruffled his hair before the boy huddled in the small nylon tent and flicked it on and off repeatedly.

Oblivious to the smiles from the other stylists and clients, Jack sat in Darcy's chair. She whipped the cape around his neck. "You really should stop giving him toys all the time."

"I don't do it all the time. Besides, it's just small stuff, and he likes it so much."

"He has an old hatbox filled with the stuff you've given him."

Jack twisted to look at her. "No kidding. Huh."

"He adores you," she said close to his ear and she got a whiff of his aftershave.

"How about his mama?"

Jack was always so blunt. She leaned forward and said, "I like you, too, Jack."

"No adoration, damn. How about that Kel Adams guy? What's he still doing hanging around?"

"Why don't you ask him?"

"I know the answer."

"Why is it bothering you so much?" He looked back over his shoulder at her. Darcy felt struck by the possessive look in his eyes. "I barely know him, Jack, but I know you. At least I think I do."

He faced front. He was quiet, his forehead furrowed as she combed and sectioned his hair, cutting on automatic since she'd been doing it for nearly two years. The silence stretched and for her own self-preservation, not wanting anyone to have something more to gossip about, Darcy turned the chair so Jack faced away from the crowd.

"Watch your back with that guy," he said after a moment.

She paused, looking at him.

"I'd hate to have to bust his chops if he hurts you."

Her champion, she thought, smiling. "You would, wouldn't you?"

His look said more than his words. "In a heartbeat."

Darcy's throat tightened, she was so moved, and she squeezed his shoulder. Jack patted her hand, saying nothing.

After a few minutes she ventured, "Jack? I need a favor, some help."

"Name it."

She blinked, not really taken aback, but reminded that Jack was one of the good guys. "I have to go to Vegas to look for someone. She's supposed to be working at a casino."

"Showgirl, croupier? Waitress?"

"Showgirl I think. A dancer, that much I know."

"What do you want to know?"

"Where would she live? What kind of area could a showgirl afford?"

"They make decent money, so the apartments past the strip would be your best bet. Easiest way is to follow the paper trail."

Darcy nodded, trimming his neckline. "I gotcha. DMV, power, phone records."

"That's a start. I've got a pal who works in Vegas, maybe he can tell you exactly where this person works." ·

"I'd rather not bother her there."

"A showgirl's schedule is tough and erratic."

"Speaking from personal knowledge?"

She caught his gaze in the mirror and that little devilish smile made her heart skip. "Maybe."

"Hand that to someone else, Jack. You've got Cheshire cat written all over your face."

He chuckled and the tension radiating between them eased a little. She finished, fluffing his hair and picking up the blow-dryer. She knew what Jack liked and kept running her fingers through his dark hair, but touching him was like adding oil to a flame and after a couple passes, she was running her hand down his jaw before she realized it. He caught her hand, looking up at her and pulling off the cutting cape.

"You keep doing that darlin' and I'll break my promise and drag you into the dark."

Her skin flushed, her body gone warm under her clothes. It felt almost instinctive to touch him. "What promise?"

"One I made to myself, not to push you where I want you to go."

She didn't ask where that would be. His expression said, bed. Long hours of hot sex. The thought made her warm all the way down to her toes, but sex with Jack wouldn't be just sex. It would be commitment, and Darcy wasn't able to do that just yet. She was a liar, a fake, and until that changed, she couldn't. But she wanted to.

The fleeting thought of Kel slipped into her mind.

How could she kiss a man in her storeroom, then in the next moment want Jack like breathing? The men were like night and day. Kel was carefree and fun loving, a big tease. Since she'd met him, she often wondered if he actually worked at his job, since she hadn't seen him do it, nor had she seen any of the pictures he'd supposedly taken of the older section of Comanche. But he always had a camera with him.

But Jack was equally handsome, yet in a totally different way. While Kel had a softer look, more *GQ,* and cared about his clothes and the statement he made, Jack had rugged, tanned features, his clothes were always a little weathered around the edges, and he spoke his mind, up-front and to the point.

And right now, she told herself, Kel Adams was safe. Jack was dangerous. He didn't do anything halfway, and once she fell, there was no turning back. She wasn't prepared to risk the relationship they had now, and was terrified of losing it if she gave in to her feelings. She wanted him, not Kel, yet they both were chasing her. It was great for her ego, but Darcy was a realist. Sex took you only so far.

Kel played. Jack played for keeps.

She brushed at his hair. "I'm done. Handsome once again."

He held her gaze for a couple seconds, not smiling, and she felt as if he was trying to delve into her mind. Then he stood and didn't even peer in the mirror, giving her an obscene tip and walking to the desk to pay. She followed him and he was already jotting something down on the back of her salon business card. He handed it to her.

"This is an old pal. Tell him I sent you, that should clear the way for anything you need."

"Thanks, Jack. I appreciate it." She didn't look at the card.

He stared at her, struggling with something. She could tell by the way his lips tightened that he wanted to say more. Then finally, he leaned forward and kissed her cheek. "Be careful, baby," he whispered softly, then left.

Darcy watched him go, which was an event in itself, then looked at Meg.

Meg grinned. "I vote for Jack."

Two stylists added a vote for Kel. She looked at Charlie, who was confused by the adult conversation and went back to playing with the penlight in the tent.

"There's no competition," Darcy said. But there was.

"Not yet," Zoe put in. "But I see one brewing."

Darcy hoped not. It was so teenage, anyway. She looked at the back of the business card.

Her features tightened.

Great. Jack's friend was a cop. Detective Kyle Windom.

Well that blows. No way was she getting anywhere near the police. Not even for help to find this Cleo Patra. She'd have to do it on her own.

With the boys in black willing to kill Tony Feeley to keep him from talking, Darcy was thinking she'd be better off with a gun.

She looked at her baby boy scribbling in a coloring book, tucked safely in his new tent. She knew she couldn't bring him along, but she'd been away from him so much lately and missed him. Leaving him with Megan was safer, she told herself. She didn't have a choice.

The music was the *ching* of slot machines, the shouts of winners. A wild assortment of people from tourists to high rollers peppered Caesar's Palace and kept the casino running at top speed.

Darcy got a little dizzy staring at all the bright lights. Her persona for the day was a high roller and she had on so much paste jewelry it was a wonder she didn't stick to the carpet. She didn't think it would do her good to look like a showgirl, since she wasn't tall enough, and the security around Caesar's Palace was phenomenal. She'd be lucky if she could get close enough to Cleo to speak with her.

Cleo wasn't hard to find. Her water bill, paid online, brought Darcy to an apartment and while Cleo wasn't there, according to the neighbors, she didn't socialize and kept late hours. Nor did she have many guests. Cleo didn't own a phone. Probably carried a cell, Darcy thought, but if it was that easy to find her, then the boys in black could, too.

Although Feeley could have been blowing smoke and could have been harassed by the thugs for another reason entirely.

The foot traffic around her was heavy. Lights sparkled like flashing beacons, luring the players and their money to the casinos beyond. She made a point not to behave as if she was searching, pausing to study the people, the restaurant menu. Her gaze shot around herself. It was instinct to stop and look, to watch her own back.

Her gaze caught on the back of a man's head. He was in the casino, moving between the blackjack tables, and something about him struck her enough for her to head that way. The crowd was heavy, brushing her hard enough for her to misstep. She peered over heads, her gaze quickly flicking over the crowd. She spotted him and moved.

Darcy was nearly close enough to get a good look, but his back was to her. It was the way he walked, she thought, not his looks.

Kel? He turned a corner, and she hurried to catch up.

But when she reached the spot where she'd seen him last, he was gone.

She looked around at the shops and restaurants, but didn't see him. The doors leading out were nearby. Giving up, Darcy turned back and headed to the Coliseum Theater. She needed to find Cleo before the show, since afterward it would be too crowded and the dancers would be making a beeline to get home.

She went into the Coliseum, marveling at the size of the place as she walked with confidence in her step, her jewelry and clothing shouting money and enough of it to burn. No one questioned her when she stepped inside the empty theater. She went up to a man who was near the stage. He was wearing a headset and carrying a clipboard, pointing to the stage and telling someone to move the lighting. Darcy assumed there was a lighting grip in the rafters.

She waited and when he noticed her, he smiled and looked her over.

"Yeah?"

"I'm looking for someone, one of your dancers."

His gaze narrowed. "What for?"

"We have a mutual friend, and they asked if I'd say hello, see how she was liking working here." Darcy put on her best fascinated face. "It looks all so exciting and glamorous," she gushed.

His gaze shot over her, noticing her designer clothing and jewelry. Darcy only hoped he didn't notice it was paste and last year's collection.

"What's her name?"

"Cleo." She cleared her throat. "Cleo Patra."

He gave her a look that was equally amused. "Yeah, she's back there." He inclined his head toward the stage door.

"May I go back?"

"Sure. They're getting ready for tonight's show."

He pressed the headset to his ear and listened, a finger up to stop her from talking. Then he frowned and spoke into the mike, "No, that's not right." He turned his back, waving her on, and Darcy drew a breath and started moving. She wasn't going to give him a chance to stop her if he had second thoughts.

She pushed through the stage doors and walked down a narrow hall that forked, one short corridor leading to the stage, the other to what she assumed was the dressing rooms. She followed the chatter, the sounds of equipment being moved. It felt familiar to her, like working on movie sets. Soon she saw people giving stage orders, and a woman who Darcy suspected was the dresser was adjusting elaborate headpieces and skimpy costumes on women who were inches taller than her, and more beautiful up close than she'd thought possible.

She tapped the dresser, who didn't even look up from working on refitting a dancer's costume. "I'm looking for Cleo."

The woman pointed off to the right and kept right

on working, straight pins in her mouth. Darcy shifted between the women and men, ignoring the stares and walking down the hall. She asked again where she'd find Cleo and a man spoke up, his gaze moving over her.

"She's in there."

"May I go in?"

He pushed away from the wall and rapped on the door, then leaned close when someone opened it a fraction. "Someone to see Cleo," he said, giving Darcy the once-over again.

The door shut and in a few minutes a black woman with flawless café-au-lait skin stepped out. She was beautiful. And really tall. She had to be near six feet, Darcy thought. It was hard to believe the woman was about forty-five.

Wrapping her silk robe a bit tighter, Cleo looked down at her, her hip cocked. "What you want, honey?"

"Can we speak in private?"

She looked around and gestured. "You see any place in this wild house?"

Darcy inclined her head and shifted away from the crowd, farther back down the hall. The click of Cleo's shoes followed her and when they were in private, she faced her.

"I'm Piper Daniels. I wanted to ask you a few questions."

She gave her a narrow, wary look. "You a cop?"

"No, I'm not."

"So what's this about? And make it quick, I've got to dress for the show and it takes a while to pack all this—" she gestured to her voluptuous body "—into half a yard of material."

"Tony Feeley said—"

"That bastard sent you?" Cleo cut in, her friendly attitude vanishing. "Forget it." She turned and headed toward her dressing room.

Darcy raced to catch her arm. "No, he didn't send me here."

Cleo looked back, losing her grip on her. "Then what do you want?"

"Information."

Cleo's beautiful kohl-lined eyes thinned. "I haven't seen Tony in years and don't want to."

"I wouldn't, either. He ranks below pond scum."

Cleo smiled slightly, yet her eyes held years of distrust. Darcy understood that. "Please, Miss Patra."

"Call me Cleo, honey. And what information do you think I have?" She lowered her voice, glancing to see if anyone was close enough to hear. "I haven't been in Tony's line of work for two decades."

"I know. This has nothing to do with Tony." Darcy debated on how to approach this, then decided straight ahead was the best way. "Twenty years ago, did you answer an ad to become a surrogate mother?"

Cleo's eyes widened, her features going slack as she stepped back, looking past Darcy and around the area.

"Sorry, sister, I don't know what you're talking about." Cleo turned and hurried down the hall.

Darcy caught up with her. "Cleo, wait."

Cleo rounded on her, nearly six feet of angry black woman towering over Darcy. "You listen to me, girl, don't come near me again, or I'll have the hotel staff kick your preppy little ass outta here."

Darcy didn't have to ask why she was so reluctant to talk. Someone was willing to kill to keep this surrogate business under wraps.

"Take this then." She handed Cleo a card with her alias and her cell number printed on it. "If you change your mind, call me."

"I won't." Crushing the card, Cleo leaned down in her face. "And if you're smart, you'll keep your mouth shut and get out of this town as fast as you can."

Cleo spun away, long curls bouncing as she stormed off.

She's scared, Darcy thought. Very scared.

Had the men who were after Tony visited Cleo?

And how was she going to convince the woman to talk to her?

Chapter 11

Cleo had been a surrogate. No doubt, after her reaction.

Walking toward the front exit, Darcy passed the ticket counter, not paying attention to anything but her own steps when she dropped her purse. She stopped to pick it up, glanced around for any loose items.

That's when she saw him. Jack. She almost didn't recognize him. He looked more like a corporate executive than a bounty hunter in the dark gray suit, dark shirt and silk tie. Hot. Incredibly polished. He was talking to a hotel staff member, handing him something.

When he lifted his gaze, Darcy felt pinned and

knew in an instant he was aware she was here. She waited till the other man left, then strode up to him.

When he looked at her, Darcy felt her insides tighten. "Did you follow me?"

He jerked his head back. "Hell, no. I knew you'd be here, but not *here*." He gestured to Caesar's.

Darcy's gaze thinned. "What are you doing here, Jack?"

"If you must *pry*," he enunciated, "I'm working on an old missing-persons case for someone. You didn't call Kyle, did you?"

"No, I didn't need to. I found her on my own."

"Good girl." He smiled.

She didn't. "Don't patronize me."

He eyed her, his smile fading. "You really think I'm tracking you?"

"Yes." He'd been outside the Match Lite Bar, and now he was here? It was too convenient.

"What the hell are you into that you'd believe that?"

"None of your business."

He stared her down. "Woman, I swear, you're stubborn enough to try a saint."

"So you keep telling me. I thought we'd settled this, Jack."

"We did. You're letting your imagination get to you."

Maybe he was right, but there were too many people moving around her life who could topple the scales.

She let out a breath. Jack moved close, moved in. She felt her insides shift and twist as he stared down at her.

"You're edgy. What's going on, Piper?"

I'm Darcy, she wanted to scream. *I'm here, can't you see me?* But she couldn't and she was so tired of it.

"Nothing I can't handle."

"You don't have to handle it alone, you know."

Yes, she did, and she wanted to share her burdens with him, but was certain he'd turn away from her. She realized Jack meant more to her than she'd thought possible.

"I do for now." She turned away and stepped outside onto the curb. He was there as she handed the valet her ticket.

"Have dinner with me later," he said suddenly.

When she looked at him, he was close. He gripped her hip, pulling her near. The air sizzled, her body suddenly aware of only *him.* Each feature, the tense strength of his muscles and the heat in his blue eyes. Before she could say a word, he kissed her. Nothing chaste and quick, but a hot, seductive slide of lips and tongue—utterly possessive, completely primal. It made her heartbeat climb rapidly, and she wanted closer.

"I accept your apology," he whispered when he drew back.

She made a frustrated sound, pushing him. "I didn't offer one." He didn't let her go just yet.

"Tasted like it to me."

Darcy smiled up at him, shaking her head.

"That's some outfit, too."

She wore a slim-fitting black sheath of lace over a flesh-colored lining.

"I can tell you're not armed, too." When she frowned, questioning, he gave her a long slow look and said, "You aren't hiding a thing in that dress."

Just then the valet pulled up. Jack stepped back to open her door. "I'm staying here."

She flicked her room key. "Paris."

His gaze lowered over her with unshielded want and he inhaled through clenched teeth. "Probably a good thing," he muttered. "Dinner, seven. I'll come for you."

"Okay."

She slid behind the wheel and smiled as she drove away. That kiss spoke volumes, and though he'd never made any overtures, his recent behavior was sending messages that were loud and clear. But she couldn't take their relationship much further. She was lying to him. And that, Jack might never forgive.

Darcy did what every red-blooded woman did in Vegas. She shopped. The fun of strolling through shops was dampened with trying to figure out how to convince Cleo to trust her. The woman had no reason to, and if Darcy were in her shoes, she wouldn't, either.

Her thoughts on a hot bath, she stepped off the elevator, then hunted in her purse for her room key. She'd taken a couple steps when she realized the hall was darker than when she'd left. She headed quickly toward her room, and just as she turned a corner someone slammed her face-first against the wall. A heartbeat later, a knifepoint dug into the side of her throat. Darcy didn't have time to be afraid.

"My money's in my purse, take it." She let it drop with the bags. He didn't go for it. She struggled and the man shoved her legs apart, nearly unbalancing her. The weight of his big body crushed her to the wall.

She smelled the minty scent of his breath as he said, "Keep your nose out of it, lady."

She didn't recognize the voice.

"You got that?"

"Sure, yeah, no problem."

He shoved harder. "You ask too many questions, bitch. Drop it or I'll drop you." He ground his crotch to her behind and revulsion floated up from her stomach. She rammed her elbow back into the man. It did nothing. Absolutely nothing. His laugh was low and cold, and he pressed the knife till a trickle of blood slid down her throat.

"Want to die now?"

"Go to hell." She drove her heel down on his foot as she threw her head back into his face. At the impact, she heard something crack.

He groaned loudly, but didn't let go. The hand in her hair slammed her forehead to the wall. Darcy saw stars and thought, *I'm going to die over this.*

Then the thunder of footsteps vibrated the floor, and seconds later the man was off her. She twisted in time to see Jack knock the blade from the man's hand and land a full-face, hammer-fisted punch right on the guy's nose. The man staggered, blood spraying from his nose. Jack didn't stop, driving his fist under the guy's chin, nearly lifting the man off his feet. Her attacker crumpled to the carpet. Jack shrugged his jacket into place and looked at her.

He was pissed. He moved toward her and instinct would have sent her backing up, but when he reached her, she let him take her into his arms.

"Thank you, Jack."

"Why'd this guy go after you?"

She pushed away from him, not meeting his gaze. "I don't know."

"Yes, you do." He tipped her chin up. "Jesus, you're bleeding."

She touched her throat, looked at the blood on her fingers. Jack gave her his handkerchief, then flipped out a cell phone and dialed. "Hotel security."

"No, Jack. Don't!"

"What? Are you crazy? It's on video." He pointed to the cameras positioned in the corners.

"I won't talk to them." She started toward her room.

He grabbed her close, his eyes sympathetic. "You won't have to. I will."

Darcy sagged, her heart pounding.

Jack spoke into the phone, his tone demanding and angry, but when he shut it off, he was calmer.

"Give me your room key."

"Why?" He flicked his fingers, not explaining. She handed it over.

He went to the room and unlocked it. "Get your stuff, you're coming with me."

"I am not."

"Yes, you are. Now. And don't give me that crap about taking care of yourself. I know you can, but tonight, you couldn't."

He waited at the door till she repacked her things.

The security was there and he wouldn't let them talk to her, giving them his cell number and telling them to take it up later. They hauled the attacker off, but not before Jack searched his pockets. No ID, no wallet. No gun. And he wasn't talking. Just bleeding.

Through the TV system, he checked her out of the hotel, then with his hand on the small of her back, he escorted Darcy out of the hotel and to his SUV. He didn't say a word. It made her nervous.

In the car she said, "Your teeth are going to be nothing but powder if you keep grinding them. Let it out."

"Let what out?"

"Your anger. I've had it directed at me before."

"You think I'm mad at you?"

"Yes."

"Christ." He pulled into Caesar's Palace, got out and tossed the keys to the valet, snatching the ticket. He shouldered her bag and nudged her along. They were alone in the elevator.

"Jack."

"Not here."

She folded her arms, glaring at him. "He-man."

"Pain in my ass." He directed her toward his room, unlocked the door and shut it behind them.

Darcy moved to the window. "Say it, whatever it is, just say it. Yell at me, whatever."

"I was scared."

She looked at him.

"To death. I didn't think I'd reach you in time."

"What?"

"I saw that guy follow you from this hotel to yours, dammit. I followed him. I missed him in the elevator and—" His gaze fell on the cut on her throat. "I thought he'd kill you."

"He didn't."

He snatched a tissue, blotting her throat. It was sealing up already. When he looked at her again, Darcy felt the air leave her lungs.

It was overpowering, the emotion in his eyes.

She turned away from it.

"You might as well tell me what you're into, because you're in way over your head."

It was true, she was. But she couldn't bring him into it, not without revealing everything she'd kept hidden for so long.

"Jack, it's my business."

"Is it? *Darcy?*"

She inhaled and went still as glass. "I don't know what you're saying."

"Darcy Allen Steele."

Her legs wouldn't hold her, her heartbeat was so fast she thought she'd pass out. She reached for the dresser, sinking to the floor, refusing to look at him, to confirm or deny. A flood of emotion and pain slipped through her like boiling water, scalding, burning.

Oh God, oh God, he knew!

"You investigated me?"

"I was a cop. A Vegas cop. And yes, I did."

"How—how long have you known?" She couldn't catch her breath.

"After I found you rescuing that woman."

"For nearly two years, and you never said anything!"

"I was waiting for you to trust me."

"It's not that simple." Still, she wouldn't look at him.

"It is now, Darcy."

She choked. Hearing her name was both painful and joyous, and the tears came, years of loneliness, of hiding and watching what she said or did chipping away like ice trapping her soul.

He was there, pulling her off the floor and into his arms, holding her tight.

Darcy cried, her fingers digging into his shoulders, arms wrapping his neck.

"Oh, Jack."

"I know, I know. It's okay, baby." His voice wavered, big hands smoothing her spine. "Take a breath."

She couldn't. It hurt.

For long moments he said nothing, simply holding her. Her shoulders jerked with each sob. He kept telling her she was safe, that he'd never let anyone hurt her again. Darcy didn't know how long she cried, didn't feel time passing, only the safe haven of Jack's arms.

"I've ruined your suit," she muttered against his chest when she'd calmed.

"It's okay. Rarely wear it anymore."

She lifted her gaze to his. "Why, Jack, why did you investigate me?"

"I wanted to make sure I wasn't doing anything illegal by helping you."

"But you were."

"Yeah, I know."

"Then why didn't you turn me in?"

His shoulders moved. "Because of you."

"As flattering as that is, there has to be more than that."

"Yeah, there is." He inhaled and exhaled as if he were about to confess a crime. "My sister was beaten to death by her boyfriend. We didn't have enough evidence for a trial and he walked. I didn't want that to happen to you." He shrugged, old pain tensing his expression. "So I watched your back."

"Oh, Jack, I'm so sorry. Is that the reason you're not a cop anymore?"

He nodded solemnly.

There was a stretch of silence, and a thousand thoughts careened through her mind. "Then you know about Maurice."

"Yes."

Shame swept her. "Oh, God." She pushed out of his arms.

"He hurt you, that's why you go after those women."

"Yes."

"You even filed charges against him, I know."

She laughed without humor. "Yes, I did. But Maurice is a very powerful man, Jack. People listened to him and not to the poor girl he married."

She couldn't believe she was telling him this, that with Jack, it was over, no more hiding, no more lies.

She sank down onto the sofa, her hands folded. "I stole my son from his father."

"You were afraid for Charlie's life."

"You have no idea."

Removing his jacket and tie, Jack went to the wet bar and poured her a drink. "I think I do, but you can tell me now, Darcy."

When he said her name, her head snapped up. He smiled. "Piper never suited you."

"I still can't believe you didn't say anything."

If she wanted proof of his trust, there it was.

"How much do you know?"

"Enough to know where you learned all those defense skills."

Athena. "Bet that was a shock."

"No, you're a strong woman."

"If I was, I would have done something about Maurice before now."

"So talk." He pushed the drink into her hand and sat beside her. "I'm listening."

Darcy heard herself speak, but it was as if she were telling a story about a part of herself that didn't exist anymore. She told him about Athena and the Cassandras, and then going to UCLA, working on movies, and meeting Maurice. Jack asked a few questions, cursed a few times, but didn't say anything more as she told him about the horrors, the abuse. Being locked in her own house for days

at a time. His features were still, but his eyes gave
him away.

She found such peace in them.

Such tender warmth and love.

And still she told him all, the shame and regret
bringing tears and anger. She told him how Rainy
had helped her escape, and how she'd taken the
burned clothing.

And when she was done bringing him up to the
present, Rainy's death, the Cassandras' investigation, and her own decision to go after Maurice, Jack
simply nodded.

"This evidence you have, the clothing, you've had
it tested?"

"No. It might be nothing."

"Doesn't sound like it. I'll have it tested."

"Jack, I can't involve you in this."

He gave her a look that said it didn't matter anymore. "You did right to have the forgeries documented, especially with Loni."

Darcy blinked.

"I worked with her in Vegas, a few years ago. You
have plenty of proof, enough to open a file on Fairchild and Steele."

"No, we don't have a body."

"We'll look. Or the cops will."

"Jack, don't you get it? I could lose Charlie over
this."

"I won't let that happen." The edge in his voice cut through the air between them. "I swear to you. Charlie is not going anywhere."

He loves my son, she thought. *He loves him.*

"How can you say that? As far as the L.A. police are concerned, Maurice is clean. I'm the criminal."

"No, you're not." Jack left the sofa and paced a little. "Even if charges were never filed against Maurice, the incident reports have to be on file. There are calls with the dispatcher. You said you have pictures. And with the servants you'll have witnesses."

"Maurice never hit me in front of anyone, Jack. He never said a cross word near a witness. The man went overboard with gifts and jewels. And I accepted them."

"Accepting them was placating his temper and we'll figure this out, together." He was quiet for a moment.

"What?" she pushed.

"If I saw you and Charlie on TV and recognized you, Steele could have seen you at that funeral, too."

"Why do you think I've been working so hard to get all this together?"

"He wants you."

"He's not getting me."

"Oh, I know that. Because you're mine."

Darcy blinked. He met her gaze, then moved across the room with quick steps as he said, "If you don't know that by now, then I'll just have to be clearer."

He reached for her. That was all it took.

Suddenly she was against him, her fingers plowing into his hair, her warm mouth moving hotly over his. His energy slammed into her, and her body fired right back like a rocket, cooking her from the inside out.

They were savage and primal, tearing at each other like starved animals. She couldn't be still, as if she had to run at top speed, nipping at his throat, his mouth, yanking his shirt from his trousers and sliding her tongue over his skin. Jack staggered, his shirt sailing to the floor. The sound of her dress zipper sliding down filled the room. He peeled it off her shoulders down to her waist.

Immediately he cupped her breasts and she pushed into his touch, begging for more as she shaped his erection trapped in his slacks. She made a little sound of hunger and passion, her kiss growing stronger. Unstoppable. As if she wanted to devour him whole.

"Oh, Jack, I knew it would be like this," she murmured against his mouth, then kissed him hotly.

"See all the time we've wasted. Tell me you really want this or I walk," he said even as he cupped her breasts, thumbed her nipples. "Because we're fast approaching liftoff."

She simply smiled, opened his slacks and freed him.

"Oh, man," he groaned as her hand closed around

his erection. She stroked him, making him tremble like a teenager, and Jack thrust into her palm.

"God, I love a woman who takes charge," he managed, his breath coming in short rasps.

Darcy felt the power of being a woman, saw it in his eyes as she slid her finger over the moist tip of him. He shuddered for her, kissing her till her legs liquefied.

"Give me everything, Jack. It's been so long." It was almost a dare, a tiny battle for pleasure and he bent, his lips closing over her nipple. She gasped, bending back over his arm and Jack flicked and suckled harder, stroking her body, dipping and rubbing between her thighs.

Darcy felt the fire inside her rupture and spread. She couldn't get enough of him, needing to feel alive and connected, even for just one night. Her hands skated over his smooth tanned skin, over ropy muscles that made her insides melt with desire. Then he moved lower, taking her dress down. Except for panties and thigh-high stockings, she was naked beneath. He licked a path down her stomach toward her center. Her body quivered with anticipation. He peeled the panties down and Darcy tipped her head back, her fingers in his hair.

Oh, I've missed this.

He spread her, driving his tongue between the folds and she flinched, then sighed with pleasure. Cupping her behind, he devoured her, sending untamed heat to the end of her nerves. Her body screamed with delight, and she gasped over and over, groping for him, pulling him back into her arms.

Mouths met and sank into each other, skin dampened, primed for sex.

"Tell me you have a condom in your wallet, cowboy," she said, shoving at his trousers. He fumbled for it, dumping his wallet on the floor, and Darcy snatched it, then hooked her foot in his slacks and sent them down. He stepped back and stripped, then grabbed her against him.

His erection pushed between them.

It was all she could do not to climb on him right now.

Then he lifted her, and she wrapped her legs around him, leaning back, and together, they tumbled to the bed. She laughed softly, clinging to him, thrusting against him.

"Now, Jack, please, oh, now."

He pressed her into the mattress, his knee wedged between her thighs. "Not so fast, baby."

"Yes, fast, right now." She squirmed beneath him, but he just grinned and dragged his tongue over her nipples, then latched on. "Ohh." She dug her fingers into his shoulders. He was devouring and greedy, and it had been so long since she felt this good. She wanted to be touched, to play and be wild with him. And he would be wild. She could feel it, in the tense yank of his body, in the way he stroked and teased her.

"Jack," she gasped.

"Man, you taste good." His mouth cruised over her skin, wet and hot. He nudged her thighs apart, slipping a finger inside her and she moaned, kissing him as he slid in and out. Her hips pumped with his touch, and when he circled the beads of her sex, she nearly came off the bed, urging him on.

Gazes locked and she cupped him, rolling the condom down, playing, making it impossible to resist her. He sat back on his haunches, scooping her off the bed and onto his lap.

She was trapped in his gaze. Everything inside her went still, hanging by a thread.

"Darcy?"

She choked.

He kissed her face. "Tell me."

"This hurts, Jack. I didn't think it would." She could feel the pain of her past shattering. A living thing that had gnawed at her for so long was dying with his touch, his trust.

"Hard to let those secrets go?" he said softly.

She nodded.

"Then let me carry them for a while."

Her eyes teared. He kissed them softly, his mouth working magic over hers and in moments the energy steamed between them, and Darcy was begging for him to be inside her.

He entered her, teasing her with the tip. "Oh, Jack."

Then in one long thrust, he filled her, making a sound all men made when they found satisfaction. Making her wounded heart bleed.

He kissed her ravenously, pushing in short thrusts, then longer and longer till Darcy felt herself falling apart inside. She moved with him, enjoying the thick hard push of man, the warm pulse inside her.

Oh, she'd missed this. She missed being taken. Feeling loved.

Her eyes suddenly burned and she scolded herself for it.

"Look at me."

She did, holding his gaze as he slid from her and then plunged deeply. He had one broad warm hand on her behind, giving her motion, the other cupping the back of her head. His eyes were bluer, intense. She'd never had a man who was so intent on her pleasure, and seeing it.

"I feel you grabbing me," he whispered, pushing harder and faster. He leaned till she was on her back, keeping his eyes on her face, the power of him pushing them across the bed with frantic cadence.

Laughing, Darcy grabbed the headboard, braced her feet on the mattress and let herself go. Her hips rose, her body open. On his knees Jack watched himself disappear into her, then met her gaze, quickening his pace. And she took all of him, a hundred sensations rushing at her at once, the feel of his skin, his fierce blue eyes, the hot throb clawing through her body. Her heart pounded wildly. Her breath labored. His hips pistoned.

"Come here, cowboy. Closer, I need you closer." Grabbing the headboard, Jack slipped one arm under her, holding her off the bed. Her spine bowed and every sensation intensified.

Faster, deeper. Hotter. He shoved once, twice. The explosion ripped through them, pleasure crashing in heavy waves. The air prickled with it, and she clamped her legs around him, pulling him down onto her as the fire roared through them like a savage beast.

Feminine muscles clamped, robbing them of thought. They strained, kissing wildly even as they tried to catch their breath. Then like a dying wind, they softened and slumped to the side, a tangle of arms and legs on a lake of wrinkled sheets.

"Ah, Jesus, Darcy," he said, breathless.

Something inside her shattered. Old pain, old life disintegrated.

She curled into his body, realized that he'd had her heart a long time ago. Tonight, she gave it freely. She met his gaze, his smile was soft and tender.

"This changes everything," she said.

He looked at her, brushing her hair back. "You okay with that?"

He seemed apprehensive right then. Darcy

cupped his jaw, laying a warm kiss over his mouth. "Yes, I am."

She settled back in his arms, her eyes closing with exhaustion and new freedom.

Then in the quiet, his voice rumbled softly. "So…you're really a blonde, huh?"

Slowly, Darcy met his amused gaze. He arched an eyebrow. She grinned, shoving a pillow in his face.

Chapter 12

In the middle of the night, Darcy's cell phone rang.

She left the bed, smiling as Jack's fingers slid over her arm.

"If that's Charlie," he said groggily, "Tell him I said hi."

"I will not. It's the middle of the night. He'll know we—" She gestured between them.

Jack grinned. "He's a smart kid, he'll figure it out."

Darcy rolled her eyes, then hunted in her purse for the phone. "Piper Daniels." Jack made a face at that.

Raspy breaths came through. "It's me."

"Cleo?"

"They came after me."

"I'm in your hotel, come right now." She gave her the room number, then ended the call.

Jack was already out of bed, pulling on jeans.

"It's Cleo, I think she's been hurt."

Darcy rifled through her bags for clothes, then went to the bath, showering quickly, then dressing. By the time she came out, Jack had everything tidy. *Got to love a man who pitches in,* she thought.

"When she gets here, don't use my real name. Just because you know doesn't mean I can afford to come out of the closet yet."

"This is getting complicated," Jack said.

When the knock came, he looked through the peephole, then said, "Jesus." He threw it open, pulling her in.

Cleo struggled against him till Darcy came to her. "It's all right, he's a friend. God, Cleo." Darcy smoothed her hair back. Cleo's face looked like a punching bag. "Jack, get some ice for this."

She led the woman to the nearest chair, and when he brought a cloth with ice, she pressed it to Cleo's cheek.

Her left eye was already darkening with a bruise, and her neck bore deep red finger marks. Big and wide. A man had tried to strangle her.

Jack offered her a glass of water, and Cleo sipped.

Darcy glanced at Jack. He didn't look happy about this and sat down beside her.

"Tell us what happened," Darcy said.

Holding the compress, Cleo gave her a one-eyed stare. "I was at my place, just got there and hadn't even opened the door yet. They came outta nowhere. One guy grabbed me and slammed me against the door. He held me by the throat, and every time he spoke, he smacked me."

"What did they want?"

"Nothing. It was just a little reminder to keep my mouth shut."

Jack went for his pistol, checking the load and putting on the holster.

Darcy knew it wasn't all because of her part in the investigation. Five other Cassandras were looking into the egg mining and Rainy's accident. She hoped they were all okay.

"I gotta go," Cleo said, trying to stand. "They'll come here and hurt you."

Darcy easily pushed her back down. "I won't let that happen."

"Neither will I," Jack said. Cleo's gaze landed on the pistol in Jack's holster. "And someone already attacked her."

"But this is the second warning," Darcy said and Jack's eyes narrowed. He'd confessed to being there as her backup when she'd met Touchy.

Slowly Cleo lowered the ice pack. "When?"

"I was meeting with Touchy and two men got to

him first. I managed to get the little pig away from them." Cleo eyed her. Darcy wasn't a big person, and clearly Cleo didn't believe that was possible. "I needed Tony alive and talking. And I'm stronger than I look."

"She kicks like a damn mule," Jack said but his look said it wasn't enough. Darcy agreed.

This was more dangerous than they'd thought and if any of it came back to hurt Charlie, she'd never forgive herself. She took a damp rag and began cleaning the cuts on Cleo's face.

"How did you get away?" Darcy asked.

"Kneed one guy in the balls, then smacked the other in the head with my purse. I have a brick in there, just for that."

"Ouch," Jack said. "Good thinking."

Darcy smiled. "How about you tell me everything?"

"What's to tell? They tried to kill me. The first man had a knife and said he was going to finish what the other man started."

"What other guy?"

Cleo looked away, then let out a harsh breath. "The one who did this." She held out her hands, palms up. Her wrists had been sliced. The scars were old and silvery. To make it look like suicide?

"Good God." Her gaze flicked up. "I think you better start from the beginning."

Cleo shook her head. "I tell you any more and you two will be in some real danger," she said. "I wouldn't risk it."

"Then why did you come here?" Jack asked.

"I had to warn you."

And she had nowhere else to go, Darcy thought. "I'm aware of how dangerous asking questions has become, but I can protect you. I can. Don't look at me like that. I do it all the time. You just have to trust me—us," she said when Jack laid his hand on her shoulder. She glanced up at him and a well of peace rose in her. He would help her. She wasn't alone anymore.

She looked at Cleo. "I can slip you into a network where no one will ever find you." She leaned close and gripped her hands. "I swear to you, we can help you."

Cleo stared for a long moment, coming to grips with trusting complete strangers, then finally nodded. Darcy went for her tape recorder, setting it on the table between them. They sat in the corner of the hotel room, Jack beside her.

Cleo looked at the recorder, then at Darcy. "I did answer that surrogate ad twenty years ago."

Darcy felt a weight slide off her shoulders.

"I wanted out of the business and I needed cash to start over. The only way to get Touchy off my ass was to promise to pay him for not working."

"Walking away from him wouldn't have been profitable to him."

"Oh, yeah, he's all about the money, the little weasel. Anyway, I called for the ad, and they sent me to a doctor. They did a physical and blood test, then they impregnated me with three embryos."

Darcy felt her hands start to sweat.

"I got pregnant with one, and they set me up in a nice apartment with strict orders to stay there and not talk to anyone about the baby." She shrugged. "I didn't know anyone, so it didn't matter. I wanted a clean break. Sitting on my butt for fifty grand was a whole lot better life than I'd had before then, so I was real game for it."

"Did they monitor you?"

"Oh, yeah, real close, and I was driven to and from Dr. Reagan's office each time by some guy who didn't talk at all."

"Reagan? You're sure?" Rainy, Justin Cohen's sister, Kelly, and now Cleo were all tied to the same dead doctor. What were the chances? Darcy thought, excitement coursing through her. "Did you notice any other women while you were in the offices? Maybe another surrogate?"

"Aside from the staff, most times there wasn't a soul in there while I was there. It was usually after normal office hours. But once I saw a girl with really clear blue eyes. I noticed her because of the color. Brilliant. She was blond, about your size, and looked sorta nervous. Like she really didn't want to be there. I heard the receptionist call her something like Tamara or Tanya."

"I wonder if she was being impregnated as a surrogate, too."

"I only saw her that one time, so I don't know if that's why she was there. Reagan was an OB-GYN, so there must have been many other women who saw him, I guess. If he did one, he could have done a lot more."

Cleo reached for the water, but her hands shook, so she set it down.

"Cleo?"

The woman looked at her.

"Did you deliver a live baby?"

"Yes, I did."

Darcy sagged into the chair. So there were potentially two children, Cleo's and Kelly Cohen's. But was either baby created from Rainy's eggs?

"When I went into labor, I called Dr. Reagan. He came and got me, but we never made it to the hospital."

"Why not?"

"A black car cut us off, and a couple guys got out. They forced Dr. Reagan from the car. They cracked him on the head and put me in their car. I wasn't in the condition to struggle. I was going to have that baby any second and I didn't care where."

"This man who took you, what did he look like?"

Cleo leaned her head back, closing her eyes and drawing on a twenty-year-old memory. "He was average, dark eyes, and I think he wore a wig. He didn't talk much and when he did, his face was sorta frozen."

"How so?"

"Like his facial muscles were paralyzed. His eyes would look angry, but his face didn't shift even a fraction. It was really creepy." She shivered. "They took me to a warehouse."

"Do you remember where it was?"

"No. I tried. It must have been somewhere near the hospital, because we didn't ride for long. But I was in hard labor and all I cared about was pushing that baby out."

"I understand that," she said, glancing at Jack. "What happened after you delivered?"

"The instant I pushed that baby out, they took her."

"Her?"

"Yeah, that much I know. It was a girl. A white baby, too. Strange. But she was so beautiful." Cleo's eyes welled up. "Pretty eyes. I never even got to touch her. Some other man took the baby. It wasn't the guy who brought me there and hurt Dr. Reagan.

This other dude, he just stood by as if waiting for a package."

This is getting more twisted, Darcy thought, checking the tape. Cleo had seen two men, one was obviously the muscle, and the second wanted the product. A human being they'd created? From Rainy's eggs, or another's?

"The guy with the wig took me back to my place. I thought he was going to kill me."

"Why would he do that? You'd fulfilled your promise."

She shook her head. "It didn't matter. As far as they were concerned I was a machine and I was no longer useful. This was some top-secret stuff. No one trusted each other. I had nightmares about what they did with the baby." Cleo shifted the ice pack, continued. "The guy held a knife to my throat, then he did this." She offered her slashed wrists as proof. "But then he helped me stop the bleeding."

Darcy's eyebrows shot up.

"Sick, ain't it? But I thought for sure I was going to die right there, so I promised not to ever talk about the baby. He told me if I did, he'd know. He'd find me and kill me. And make it hurt."

"Did Dr. Reagan ever come to you?"

"Yeah, Dr. Reagan came to the apartment with some other guy. I heard him call him Peters. They asked me what happened, and all I said was that the baby was kidnapped. I told them those other guys drugged me and that I didn't remember even having the baby. I didn't even tell them it was a girl."

"Do you think they believed you?" Jack asked.

"I don't care if they did and I didn't ask. They were pissed. I gave them back most of the money and left town fast."

"This man, Peters. Was he a doctor? Can you describe him for me?"

Cleo looked at the notepad, then Darcy. "He was older, maybe sixty, sixty-five. Tall, skinny, with snow-white hair. I don't remember his eyes, he stayed back from me like I had some disease or something. He had a lot of creases in his face and acted real superior, like he was better than anyone on the planet and Dr. Reagan was his flunky. He wasn't concerned that the baby could have been harmed or killed or that I was cut up."

Cleo clamped her lips shut, her smooth forehead knitting.

"What are you thinking?"

"I'm thinking he was the boss. Because Dr. Reagan did whatever he said. Dr. Reagan checked me to see if I was okay, you know, after the birth and my wrists, but the Peters guy was annoyed and impatient."

"Has anyone besides me and the bastards who did that—" she pointed to the new bruises and cuts "—ever contacted you since then?"

"No, not outright. But they've been around."

"Really. Did you see them? Did they send a message or something?"

"No, they never talked, never called or nothing, but I was a hooker, I can spot a cop or someone who doesn't belong somewhere real fast." She snapped her fingers. "And once in a while I'd see some guy hanging around, smoking a joint on the street corner or drinking with the winos, watching me. And I knew they weren't part of the crowd, you dig?"

"Yeah, I dig." It was why Darcy used disguises and makeup and had for years watched the way people behaved. She'd pattern herself after someone she'd seen and slide into the role.

"Did you see anyone else besides that one girl at the doctor's office, a technician maybe or a nurse?" Darcy thought if she could pinpoint someone working there back then, she might be able to get more information on how and why Reagan had done this. Clearly, he'd been the one to harvest the eggs, or at least given someone a heads-up on a prime candidate to harvest.

"Yeah. Reagan had an assistant, a nurse. She wasn't there all the time. Maybe two or three. Late forties, blond hair with bad roots and blue eyes."

"A name?" Though she could have told Cleo herself.

Cleo thought for a second. "Stand...no, Stone."

Darcy's features pulled taut. She looked at Jack and stood.

"You've made a connection," Jack said.

"Yes, to Athena. Betsy Stone is the Academy's nurse."

"You need to warn your friends."

"I will when we get home, but first we have to get Cleo to a safe place. She's the only one so far who can confirm that there were surrogates and they were connected to Betsy Stone and Dr. Reagan."

Jack stared down at her, his hands on her arms. "You need to contact the police."

"I can't. Not yet. It's not up to me alone, Jack. The Cassandras have to be told all this first. But I have to get Cleo into hiding."

He agreed, reluctantly. "I didn't want that badge back, anyway."

"Oh, jeez, Jack. Don't get involved if it will ruin you."

"We're in this together now, baby." He rubbed her arms, his voice low, almost intimate. "Your friends, these Cassandras, they know about what Maurice did to you?"

"They hadn't back then. Only Rainy did. I was too ashamed to admit it or get them involved. I think they've guessed, though. Kayla knows some of it. Alex, too, I think."

"You need to talk to them, baby. They're your friends."

"I—I will."

"I'll be there if you want."

She smiled, touched. "Thanks, Jack. But that will wait. We have to get organized. I need the case out of the back of my trunk."

"Makeup?"

She nodded and started dialing the network. She looked at Cleo. "We have to get you hidden, deep. You can't go back to your apartment."

"What about money? I have money."

"Got an ATM card?" Jack asked and Cleo nodded. "Give me the number and I'll draw out money for you. They'll be looking for you two, not me."

Cleo handed it over. "I'm trusting you with my savings." She gave him an amount to take out.

"I'll be back in a few, there's a machine downstairs." Jack slipped on a jacket, then kissed Darcy.

"Get some clothes, Jack, men's clothing, too. I can't disguise her well, but we can make it less obvious that she's a showgirl."

Jack glanced at Cleo's long legs and short skirt. "That will take some doing. I won't be long."

When she locked the door after him, Cleo said, "He's cute. You love him?"

She blinked. "I don't know." Did she?

"He loves you."

"What makes you say that?"

"He never questioned you, doubted you, and now he's risking his life for you. Girl, that's love."

Darcy allowed herself a small smile, then went to work, packing everything up and dialing the network again. She couldn't get anyone to answer and there wasn't a machine to leave a message. She wished Jack would return, but she knew he had to go someplace else for the clothes besides the hotel stores. Armani wasn't in the budget.

"It's hard to believe that someone wants to kill me because I had a baby."

Darcy related. There was nothing more horrifying than to know that someone actually wanted you *dead*. It had a startling effect, making her want to fight the very idea. She hoped Cleo was ready to do the same. There was no turning back. Whoever had taken the baby was willing to kill to keep it quiet. Rainy had been the first to pay the price. As far as Darcy could see, they were all becoming expendable.

Someone jiggled the door handle. Darcy stilled, moving to peer through the peephole. She couldn't see anyone, but a shadow moved against the far wall. As if the person knew he'd be seen through the peephole. She drew her knife, wishing there was a window. Someone pushed on the handle and Darcy looked again. A figure moved away.

It wasn't Jack, but he was big.

She backed away from the door, tense. She heard something in the room next door and thought, had they just misjudged the room number?

"Why are you doing this for me?" Cleo said softly.

Darcy pressed her ear to the wall, listening. No sound. "Because you're in trouble. You don't deserve to be, you had a baby thinking it was for some childless couple and you got the rotten end of the deal."

"There is something else you two are not saying, though. Or you wouldn't have come looking for me. I think I have a right to know the whole story."

"Yes, you're right, you do deserve to know, but it's dangerous," Darcy said. She looked out the peephole, saw nothing and stepped away.

"They want to kill me. How much more dangerous could it get?"

"I see your point." Darcy told her about Rainy, and the discovery of the egg mining. Cleo's eyes widened as she filled her in on the Athena Academy grads' theory.

"I had this woman's child? This Rainy Miller Carrington?"

"Unless there are more women who were used, it's entirely possible you could have given birth to a child created from her eggs. Eggs that were fertilized with some man's sperm."

"And you think they killed her because she found out these people had taken her eggs when she was a kid?"

"No doubt about it."

"Jesus Christ," she muttered. "What did they do with the baby? Hell, she'd have to be about twenty years old now."

"I don't know. My friends and I are all looking into this, but we've barely scratched the surface. I'm going to hide you, Cleo, but you have to stay connected to only me. When we do learn the truth, we might need you to testify. You cool with that?"

Cleo snapped her fingers and did what Darcy referred to as "the home girl head slide." "In a heartbeat."

An unexpected rap on the door startled them, and they both froze. Darcy grabbed her knife, and whispered, "Get back out of sight."

Cleo went into the bathroom, closing the door.

With her knife behind her back, she looked through the peephole, expecting housekeeping. She got Jack.

She opened the door.

He looked at the knife. "You need a gun." He pushed his way in.

"I hate them. Besides, they look better on you."

Darcy went to the bathroom, letting Cleo out. Jack handed the bags to Cleo, then an envelope of money and her cards. Cleo smiled, but counted it, checked it against the receipt. Jack was amused.

Cleo sifted through the clothes, holding them against herself to check the size. "Decent," she said, then folded them.

"Get changed," Darcy said, then to Jack, "Where's the makeup kit?"

"Couldn't get to it and it won't matter, we're getting out of here now. I spotted company downstairs. Someone was asking about her."

"Someone just tried the doorknob. I thought it was housekeeping."

"I'm betting it wasn't."

Darcy trusted his judgment.

"I'm checked out, we take the bags and get lost, fast. Did you contact the network?"

"I can't get anyone to answer." It was making her nervous.

When Cleo came out, they were ready.

"We go down the back stairs to the garage floor," Jack said.

Darcy agreed. "Were they headed up here?"

"They got an ID on her, so yeah. We have about two minutes before they're on this floor." Jack looked out into the hall. "We have to make a run for it."

"Oh, jeez," Cleo said, tucked behind them.

"There's a stairwell to the left. I want you to go

first, then Cleo. I'll be right behind you. Go to my car, I'll come back for yours later."

With her knives in easy access, Darcy stepped out. She looked left and right, then to Jack. He pushed them both ahead. "Go, go."

They trotted down the steps, the echo in the stairwell making too much noise. They had to cover several floors and by the time they reached the last they were breathing hard and sweating. The bags felt like boulders.

Cleo jumped the last four steps.

Jack peered through the small wired-glass window leading to the parking area. "I'm parked in the far corner near the service elevator." Jack opened the door, motioning to them and the women stepped out, heading straight to the car. Jack pinched the key ring, the car locks sprang and headlights blazed bright in the darkness. "Hurry, ladies!"

Darcy tossed the cases in beside Cleo, as Jack slid behind the wheel and started the engine. Locking her seat belt, she looked in the rearview mirror and saw two men, running, aiming guns.

"Oh, no, Jack. Move!" One was the man who'd attacked her!

"I see them. How'd the little bastard get out of jail already? Get down."

Throwing the car in reverse, Jack hit the car alarm,

the loud, constant pulse echoing through the parking garage as he backed out. He clipped a parked car, shifted, then slammed his foot on the gas. Gunshots blasted, one plunking into the side of the car.

"Cleo!" Jack swerved the car. "Cleo!"

Darcy twisted in the seat. "She's okay, Jack."

"Oh, God, the bullet's in the door, right beside me!"

"Dammit, who are these people?" Darcy snapped.

Jack handed her his gun. "If they shoot, shoot back. Aim low, at the tires."

Darcy swallowed, taking the gun, and glanced in the side mirrors. A black sedan was damn near kissing the bumper. Jack took a curve and gunned the engine harder, bouncing up the car-lined corridor, the bottom of the car hitting the pavement and sending up a burst of sparks. The car fishtailed to the right, and he corrected, the vehicle swerving before it lurched out of the garage and into the street like Jonah spit from the whale.

Cars swerved to avoid them and he headed toward the highway. It was the only way they could lose them.

"Shoot!"

Darcy opened the window, leaning out.

This is not as easy as it looks on TV, she thought. She pulled the trigger and the car behind them swerved hard.

Jack jammed on the gas and Darcy fell back into the seat.

Cleo was looking out the back window and slowly brought her gaze to Darcy. "Nice shot, girl."

Darcy handed Jack back the gun as if it was infected.

"Well, we know one thing," Jack said.

Darcy looked at him. His gaze was shooting all over, the mirrors, the road, then her. "Whoever orchestrated Rainy Miller's death is out to make certain no one knows why."

Chapter 13

The egg mining conspiracy, as Darcy had come think of it, knew where Cleo had been all this time. They'd watched her, noticed who she'd spoken with and Darcy realized that contacting Tony "Touchy" Feeley had put them on Cleo's trail again. And on hers.

Darcy could kick herself.

She'd hidden from Maurice, kept much of her life from her Athena sisters and now she was on the verge of losing everything. More people would be hurt, she thought with a glance at Cleo asleep in the seat behind her.

Jack seemed to sense her anxiety and reached out, covered her hand and squeezed. "We'll make it."

Darcy could only nod, then pulled out her cell and dialed one of her contacts. She didn't have time for the safe house. It was too far away. She had to hide Cleo tonight. She couldn't risk a tail to her home, her business. She waited for Steve or Krissie Bishop to pick up.

"I have a package."

"Jeez, Piper, don't you ever rest?" Steve said, grouchy.

"Life happens all the time," she said and regretted her waspish tone. "Sorry. This is major. My package has to go deep. Now."

Behind her, Cleo roused, listening.

"No, I don't have time for the usual routes. Or a good cover." She listened as Steven Bishop gave her options. They would take her under if she got Cleo to the change point, a warehouse that Steve and Krissie had set up to house women while Steve made new IDs for them.

Darcy checked her watch, then glanced at the mileage road sign. "In the late afternoon. It will take me that long and I have to cover my tracks. Great." She cut the line, laying the phone on the console.

"Whazzup, girl?"

Darcy met Jack's gaze, then looked at Cleo. "I'm going to hide you for a while. You won't be able to work, but these people will help you stay safe."

"I need to work, Piper."

Darcy didn't correct her name. The less anyone knew, the better. "I know, but consider that your life is at risk. Make a choice."

Cleo sighed hard. "You're right. But doing nothing's going to make me crazy. What can I contribute?"

"What are you good at?"

"Besides shaking my ass to music, not much."

Jack laughed shortly and kept driving. "Ass shaking is a good living I hear," he said.

"Yeah, but I have money now. I've saved for years. I wanted to marry, retire and have my own babies."

Darcy smiled sympathetically. Regardless of the circumstances of the pregnancy, it couldn't have been easy losing the child, especially knowing that people ruthless enough to cut her wrists had the baby.

"It'll be all right, Cleo. We'll find the child and get the bastards who hurt you."

"You think?" Cleo scoffed, not at all convinced.

"I know." Determination strengthened her tone. "But you can't touch the rest of your money or go home after today, or they'll know. Maybe we can get someone to go back if there's something important you need, but for now, all ties have to be cut. I can't be certain but I have a feeling these people have their fingers in networks that I can't even imagine."

Cleo shifted, sighing. "Well, I'm good with computers."

"Really? You don't strike me as the computer-geek type."

"Hey, geeks are cool." She flashed her a smile. "I didn't go out much, so yeah, I can find my way around a computer."

"Good, but don't touch your accounts, credit cards, nothing. You won't need to. My friends will put you to work, trust me."

Cleo nodded, agreeing to the terms that would change her entire life for God knew how long.

Jack drove without stopping. Darcy made a call to the Bishops and directed Jack to a warehouse. As they approached, the huge door rolled up. Once they were inside, it shut and the lights came on. Krissie and Steven Bishop walked out.

Darcy and Jack climbed out. Steve was walking toward her till he saw Jack and stopped short.

"Turner?"

"Hello, Bishop."

Darcy frowned between the two men. Steve Bishop was an ex-cop. His wife had been a dispatcher. They were the heartbeat of the network, moving women from here to the safe houses. The last time she'd seen them was with Mary Jo.

"You know each other?" Darcy asked.

Jack slid her a glance. "Yeah. We went to the academy together. I'm not on the force anymore, Steve."

"How'd she get you into this?"

"Osmosis, I guess." Jack winked at Darcy.

Cleo climbed out, looking around and drawing attention. Darcy introduced her.

Bright and always cheery, Krissie nudged past her husband, saying, "You can stay with us, help out here till we can move deeper. There is no place safer right now, Cleo. We'll give you a new identity, but I think it's best if you stay out of sight." She glanced at Darcy for confirmation, then looked back at Cleo. "Sorry, but as a woman, you're just too tall to go around unnoticed."

Darcy didn't tell the Bishops that Cleo was a showgirl. That was Cleo's choice. All they knew was that Cleo had to hide, yet had to be accessible to Darcy. She didn't give details, yet she was certain Alex or Kayla would want to interview Cleo, and knowing Tory, she'd want to document the entire investigation. It was safer if only Darcy knew where Cleo was.

"You okay with that?" Darcy said to Cleo.

"Anything is better than dead, thank you."

Darcy smiled, then looked at Steve. "By the way, Cleo knows computers."

He clutched his chest. "Woman after my own heart."

Krissie groaned. "Oh goody, another one who talks in megabytes."

Smiling, Steve nodded toward the setup in the loft. "Come on, let's get you a new identity, and I'll show you around."

Jack moved up beside Darcy and she looked at him. "So this is how you get it all done, the fake IDs?"

"Yeah. There are a few more stations like this, but this is where the most work is done. Are you mad?"

"No, but I can see several violations from here."

She groaned. "I know, Jack. Why do you think I wanted to keep you out of this?"

"I understand, but it scares the hell out of me that you take risks like this."

Cleo walked toward them and stared at Darcy. "You okay?" Darcy asked.

"Thanks. I feel safe for the first time in a long while." Cleo reached out, hugging Darcy and nearly bringing her off the floor. "Thank you so much. I'd be dead without your help, and I won't forget that."

Darcy held tight, liking the woman and praying this all worked out before anyone else got hurt. "Do what they say, Cleo," she said when they parted. Her eyes burned. "If they need to move you somewhere else, do it. This is my number." She gave her another card with her number. "Memorize it. And if you need me or think anyone's getting close, call me. I'll come to you."

"My own personal cavalry, huh?" Cleo pushed the card inside her bra.

Darcy smiled, reaching for Jack's hand. "You could say so."

"You and your friends will keep looking for the child?"

"Yeah, we will." Whether the child Cleo had carried was Rainy's or not didn't matter right now. Matching up DNA when and if they found the girl would give them the answer. But it was the conspiracy, the entire manipulation of Athena Academy, its resources and the students, that needed to be uncovered. The trouble she'd encountered already told Darcy that this was more widespread than any of them thought. There could be other babies…well grown women or men now, that had been created by these people. The biggest question still was, *why?*

"Stay cool, sister." Cleo gave her a straight-arm tap on the shoulder, then turned away.

Krissie walked up. "Jack's a good man."

"I know, Krissie, I know."

She and Jack said goodbye and got back in the car. Steve climbed the ladder on the warehouse wall near the doors, then checked the area before he opened the door. They drove out sedately.

Darcy would have liked to see Cleo at the safe house in Utah, but too many people lived there, and Cleo's physical appearance was harder to disguise. Although the network had operated in secret for years, Darcy couldn't risk Cleo's life. She was the first tangible witness to the conspiracy.

If anyone found her, they'd kill her.

When Darcy and Jack arrived at her place, it was late afternoon. Megan was at the house, and when Charlie saw her, he flew at her. Then Jack walked in and Darcy was suddenly ignored. Megan walked up beside her and they both watched Charlie and Jack. "So does Jack still get my vote?"

"Oh, yeah."

"Ah, I haven't seen that look on you before."

Darcy didn't comment on the smile she had when Jack was near. Was it a feeling of relief or something more? "He knew who I was all this time, Meg."

Megan blinked. "Oh, hell."

"He gets the good-guy award for that, huh?"

"What about Kel?"

"I'll break it off with him tomorrow. I have to call the Cassandras and tell them what happened first."

"You were missed at the shop. Mrs. Burkewater is complaining."

"Mrs. Burkewater always complains. I'll take care of her on Tuesday, give her twenty percent off. She'll love it." Darcy hated being away from her salon, but with all the girls working for her, she didn't have to be there. She did have to be there for Charlie, though.

Megan leaned closer to whisper, "Kel was in looking for you, by the way."

"When?"

"The day you left for Vegas."

He knew she was there, Charlie had said as much to him. Her gaze moved to Jack, and she wondered if she should tell him about seeing Kel in Vegas. Or rather, that she *thought* she'd seen Kel. And if he'd been there, why hadn't he made himself known?

Jack's cell phone buzzed and he answered it, setting Charlie down. She heard him curse under his breath.

"Give it to someone else."

Darcy moved to him, covering the phone. "When?"

"Tomorrow. It's a lead on a bounty headed west to California."

"Take it, we'll be fine. Right here."

Jack muttered into the phone and shut if off. "I don't like this. It's different now."

"Between you and me, yes, but between Maurice and me, it's the same, and with the Cassandras. I have to tell them tonight, Jack. Everything. Besides, you can't just suddenly stop your life for me."

"I would to keep you safe, Darcy."

A little tickle of giddy pleasure shot through her every time he said her name.

Charlie tugged on Jack's pant leg. He looked down. "Are you staying?"

Jack looked at Darcy as if waiting for her to say something.

"Yes, Charlie, he is."

Charlie whooped, and on the other side of the room, Megan smiled, folding her arms across her skinny middle. "It's about damn time."

Jack wouldn't leave to go after his bounty until he saw the evidence she had on Maurice. She gave it all to him and he sifted through it like a detective, laying out each component and making notes.

"The clothes, where are they?"

She went to the freezer and gave him the bag.

Jack broke the seal, sniffing. His head jerked back. "Christ, that's strong."

"I know, raunchy. I don't know what it is, though."

Jack snipped a sample. "I'll have it tested."

"Calling in old cop favors for me, I'm touched."

He flashed her a smile and when she passed him, he pulled her onto his lap.

"You've got a lot here, Darcy. The handwriting forensics are complete and documented. That'll be your biggest weapon. Loni Marks's verifications. It's solid admissible evidence of forgery. On the surface, you could turn it over and it would lead police right to Maurice and a conviction."

"But that's not enough, Jack. He could pay his way out of a forgery charge."

He scowled. "Your lack of faith in the justice system is almost insulting."

"Do you blame me?" He kissed away any argument. "I know in my gut he killed that woman. If I could find a body—"

"I'll say again, let the cops handle this stuff. You have the bloody clothes with Maurice's DNA on them, plus, if your theory is right, the victim's DNA."

She was certain it was Porche's. Her gaze slipped to the bag of clothing, and she left his lap and opened it. She sniffed the fabric again. "That's not charred fabric, it's chemical. Not a fragrance, though." And it was familiar. Just on the edge of her memory.

She sat still, closing her eyes and thinking. Occasionally she took a whiff of the evidence bags. Her mind ticked off her career in the movie business, plucking through each movie set she'd worked on, each actor she'd had to dress and make up.

"Stop that, you're going to kill brain cells," Jack said, breaking off her train of thought.

He stored the evidence and boxed it up. "I'm taking this."

"Why?"

"I'll give it to someone who can make a case."

When she looked apprehensive, he came to her. "Do you trust me?"

"Yes," she said instantly.

"Then you have to let the legal system work for you."

"And if it doesn't? If I go to jail for taking Charlie?"

"I won't let that happen. Charlie means everything to me, too, and I'll hide out forever with you if it comes to that."

Darcy looked up into his Nordic blue eyes and for the second time in a week, laid her trust in his hands.

The Cassandras had answered her e-mail for the conference call. Kayla, Alex, Josie and Tory were on the line. Samantha St. John, a CIA operative, had responded via e-mail that she couldn't call but to fill her in on everything. Megan sat beside Darcy, her moral support as always.

"You've got us scared, Darcy, you okay?" Kayla said, her voice clear through the speakerphone.

"I'm sorry. This is important. I should have told you all years ago, but I just couldn't."

"Is this about your new hair color and why you disappeared at the funeral when the press was there?" Alex said.

The comment didn't surprise her, they were in tune with each other, even after all this time.

"Yes." Darcy took a deep breath and began. She withheld nothing, not a single detail of her life with Maurice. They'd all been at the wedding. Poor girl marries millionaire. It sounded good. She was crying by the time she got to the night Rainy came for her, and had to stop to collect herself. She apologized for hiding all this. But she was ashamed, mortally ashamed of her weakness. There was a stretch of silence. Darcy looked at Megan, uncertain.

Then one clear voice, Kayla, said, "Rainy told me some of what you've been through. We all guessed that something was wrong with your marriage. We knew you would come to us when you were ready. You want us to go after him?" They started chattering at once, agreeing.

Darcy deflated into the chair, relieved beyond measure. She wiped her eyes and smiled. "I love you all, you know that."

"Oh, Darcy, what a burden this must have been all this time," Josie said. "And with Charlie to protect, too."

"We've all made mistakes," Tory said. "It's not your fault. Fear for your life is not a flaw."

When they asked about what she planned now, Darcy explained the situation with Porche Fairchild. They all had input that gave her confidence. She wasn't alone anymore, and she realized that her life would have been so much easier if she'd just told them the whole truth from the start. Shame was an ugly thing, she thought.

"I can test the clothing if you want," Alex offered.

"I could run a check on Fairchild, see if she has prints on file," Kayla said.

They each offered help and Darcy felt her soul lift.

Alex said, "That evidence might not stand up in court because it wasn't collected by forensics."

"I know that. It's a chance I have to take." But she wasn't dispirited.

"One more thing."

"There's more?"

"I found a surrogate."

"Way to go!" came through the speakerphone. She explained about finding Touchy, the boys in black, and Cleo Patra. She told them what had happened in Vegas and all she'd learned from Cleo. "Dr. Reagan and Betsy Stone are the connections to Cleo and this Peters guy. Maybe if we find Reagan's records they'll lead us to Peters."

"Where is Cleo now? I'd like to talk to her," Tory said.

"I have her hidden. She told me everything she could and until I know it's safe, no one can go near her. I'll copy the tape recording and send one to each of you. But considering they chased us down and shot at us, we can't let anyone know we have her."

"You really need to carry a gun, Darcy."

Darcy sank back into the cushions. "You sound like Jack."

"Who's Jack?" Josie asked curiously.

"A bounty hunter."

"Intriguing." This from Kayla.

She glanced at Meg, who was smug. "He is," she said and Darcy introduced her trusted friend to the Cassandras. They all thanked her for being Darcy's friend and support.

"Can you count on this Jack for help?"

"Yes," she said without hesitation. "Jack knows everything. In fact he's known who I am for nearly two years and kept his mouth shut."

"I like him already." Darcy thought that was Josie.

"We want to help, Darcy," Alex said.

"You can't." When they all protested Darcy reminded them, "I'm a parental kidnapper, ladies. I don't want any of you accused of aiding and abetting."

"But you'll let this Jack help?"

"Jack isn't a man who takes no for an answer."

She wondered how he'd feel about her going to see Kel. She had to, it was only fair to break off what little relationship they had. Besides, she wanted to confront him about seeing him in Vegas. She still wasn't sure if it had been him, since she never got a good look.

But Darcy trusted her instincts and so far they hadn't steered wrong.

Chapter 14

Darcy found it odd that the instant Jack left her house, Kel called, inviting her over for a drink. She agreed for one reason only—to say goodbye.

Her cell rang just as she knocked on Kel's door. She answered it. "Yes, you can have cookies and milk tonight and mind your manners." Kel opened the door, smiling.

"Charles?" he asked.

She nodded, said goodbye and ended the call. "He's excited about watching some new video."

He took her jacket, hanging it up on a peg near the door. He kissed her softly, running his hand down her back. She stepped away, wondering why his touch didn't evoke the same feelings as before. *Jack,* she thought, walking farther into the apartment.

"This is cute." It was sparse, a studio of sorts, with only a partition wall hiding the bed. It must have come furnished, she thought. It looked generic.

There wasn't a radio but a small TV that looked like a throwback from the eighties sat in the corner of the living area. Not his, she decided. His camera equipment was set up in the corner, one camera on a tripod, and photos lay strewn on the table.

"May I?" she asked, pointing.

"Sure."

She picked up a stack, examining them as he took out two wineglasses. The photos were lovely. Sunsets, old homes, the city from the hilltop. Like postcards.

"These are very nice."

"You're too kind. They're just preliminary shots. Seeing what I like the best, then I'll go back and shoot again to narrow it down. They don't pay for so-so, only for the spectacular."

She heard the pop of a cork, and looked up.

He held up the bottle. "Wine?"

"I don't drink." Her mother was an alcoholic. She'd seen the effect up close and personal.

"I love American wines." He showed her the label. "Costs a fortune in England. You sure you won't have some? You look as if you could use some relaxation."

Laying down her purse on the sofa, she went into the kitchen. When he put the wine in the fridge, she added, "I'll have one of those, though."

She pointed to the bottled iced tea, noticing everything in one sweep. The worn appliances and dishes that must have come with the place, the fridge that had little in it except what he'd recently purchased. What really got her notice was that his clothes were still in a suitcase instead of the dresser. There wasn't any paraphernalia on the dresser, no jewelry, aftershave, receipts, pocket change.

He poured the tea into a glass, then handed it to her. Darcy drank half of it, not moving when he motioned her to the living-room area.

"I can't stay, Kel. I came here for one reason."

He frowned. "Well that doesn't sound good."

"We can't see each other anymore."

"And here I thought it was going great."

"It was nice, but you're leaving the area and I don't want it to go further."

"It's him, isn't it? That bulldog, Jack Turner."

"That's none of your business."

"You could at least have the decency to tell me the truth."

"Fine, it is Jack." She tripped over the words, her mouth suddenly numb. She frowned down at the iced tea, then peered at the bottom of the glass. A faint swirl of greenish powder colored the bottom.

Her gaze snapped up. "You drugged me."

His look was deadpan. "I beg your pardon?"

"There's something in this."

"You're imagining things."

Oh, no, Darcy thought, feeling her limbs soften.

"What the hell did you do?" She turned away, and grabbed the table when her world tilted. "Who the *hell* are you?!"

"If you must know, I'm an actor."

Darcy's heart slammed to a stop and she choked for air. Oh, no. Maurice!

"Ah, I see you understand."

"You bastard." She tried to move around the edge of the counter, ready to tear him apart, but he sidestepped and she nearly fell. The numbing feeling seeped down her body like liquid fire. She reached for her knife, turning to throw, but he knocked it out of her hand, shoving her onto the sofa.

"No, it's your husband who's the bastard."

She grappled for purchase. Her bones felt liquefied.

"Let me help you to the sofa." His accent was completely gone.

"Drop dead." She looked at him, blinked, then sent her fist driving into his face. The impact rang up her arm and sent him flying backward. She struggled to her feet, the room swaying. She had to get out of here.

"Well I didn't expect that, Mrs. Steele." He worked his jaw, spit blood.

"I'm going to kill you," she said, her words slurred, yet holding the power of her rage. Suddenly, her legs folded and Darcy dropped to the floor.

"I'll be out of the country by the time you wake up."

"You have no idea what you're dealing with, Kel, or whoever you are!"

"Yes, I do. Your husband is a very powerful man in Hollywood."

"You owed him, didn't you?"

Kel's expression sharpened. "Yes, I did. He got me out of a jam a couple years back." His tone went bitter. "I've been paying for it for some time now. But my career means more to me."

Her world moved along in slow motion, faint sounds amplified, and she barely managed, "Ho-how did he find me?" Did it matter now? She tried pushing herself up off the floor, but her arms wouldn't obey her mind.

"The news report, ABS. About some funeral. Charlie and you were on it. He hired a detective to find you, then sent me in to hook you."

Rainy's funeral. Ex-Athena student Shannon Connor had blasted Athena Academy in that news report. Mostly because Shannon had a grudge against Athena and the Cassandras. She'd tried to frame

Josie for stealing. Tory had exposed her, and Shannon had become the only student ever to be expelled from Athena.

Shannon must have caught her and Charlie on film at the funeral. Maurice knew she wouldn't have missed the service. He must have recognized her and tracked her and Charlie through their plane tickets, must have discovered her alias.

This is my fault. I knew it was coming and didn't move fast enough!

Kel picked up her purse, digging in it and Darcy's panic shot like a rocket through her when he pulled out her cell phone. Kneeling near her, he hit Star 69, then dialed the last number. She could barely hear Megan answer, saying her whole name. Meg had no fears; her common-law husband was behind bars for the rest of his life for murder. Kel cut the line, then dialed information, asking for an address. "Clever girl, hiding him with your receptionist."

Angry tears burned her eyes. Charlie, oh God, *my baby*. Maurice would use him for the single reason that Darcy loved him more than her own life.

Kel bent and gripped her jaw, kissing her roughly. "It was fun while it lasted, love." He stood.

The drugs kicked through her, narrowed her vision, paralyzing her arms and legs. She could feel her heartbeat slow down.

Kel's footsteps and the slamming door echoed through her mind.

Then everything went black.

Maurice's jet landed at a small airport outside Comanche. Kel was waiting for him beside a compact car.

"Be gassed and ready to go in a moment," Maurice said to the crew as he stepped onto the flight deck. He took one look at the small car and made a face.

He got in. "You couldn't do better than this roller skate?"

Kel met his gaze. "A limousine will be noticed."

Maurice flicked a hand for him to drive. "She's out cold, correct?"

"Yes, for at least eight hours."

"Good work. Let's get the boy."

"He's with the receptionist."

Maurice sent him a hard glance. "You don't have him?"

"She hid him from everyone. No one knew who cared for the kid while she was away. And you wanted to do this. I said I'd find her and get close to her, but I'm not stealing the kid. That's a felony."

"And you do have a sexual assault record, don't you?"

Kel's expression turned bitter. "You better make this worth it, Steel."

"Or?"

"I'm not sure. If you'd been here when I called, I might have found the boy sooner while she was in Vegas."

"I had appointments I couldn't break." Maurice gave a distasteful look at the passing scenery. "Did you ever learn what she was doing there?"

"No. She almost spotted me, so I disappeared."

Maurice gave him an annoyed look and when the car pulled into the driveway of a small house, he got out and with determined steps went right up to the door. He didn't knock, and pushed his way in.

Darcy was abruptly aware of her surroundings.

Her face was hot, her skin itching. It felt like ants crawling over her back, making her shift and pushing back the thick, cottony feeling in her brain.

Sprawled on the floor, she had no idea how much time had passed.

Charlie.

The thought of her son in danger forced her to move her legs, draw her arms to support herself as she pushed up on her hands and knees. Her stomach recoiled and she gasped for air, trying not to retch and then not caring. Bile spilled, burning her throat. Crap. She swiped her mouth and struggled to her feet.

Her knees went soft and she grabbed the sofa arm, lurching into it. She lay there for a minute, trying to breathe, to clear the cloud of drugs. *What did he give me?* Now that it was out of her body, after a couple minutes, her blurry vision began to clear. Her breathing sounded like an engine in the small apartment.

She looked around. Alone.

Her heart twisted with anger and worry, and she grabbed the phone. No dial tone. Staggering to her feet, she swallowed, her mouth dry. She ripped the place apart looking for her cell phone. She found it in Kel's suitcase along with papers from Maurice. An investigator's report. She tried reading them but the words swam like bugs on the page. Stuffing them in her jacket, she dialed Meg. All she got was a busy signal.

Darcy cursed, the floor feeling unstable beneath her feet as she hurried to the sink. Filling a glass of water, she drank, then shoved her head under the faucet. *Charlie,* repeated in her mind, her thoughts going wild over what Kel would do with her son.

I'll kill him. I swear to God, I will kill him.

She shook her head like a dog, smoothing her hair back as she looked out the window. The break of dawn painted the night sky purple. *It's been hours.* Charlie would be scared. He'd scream. Maurice needed Charlie unharmed, but Darcy feared Kel had hurt Meg to get him. Her friend wouldn't give up Charlie without a fight.

She dialed 911 and told the police that she'd been drugged against her will and where they'd find the evidence. She gave them the address, said Kel had done it to kidnap her son. They'd send a car to her house, but Darcy knew it was too late. It had been hours. The police wanted her to wait where she was. All she said was "No" and cut the line.

Whoever Kel really was, he was going to jail. And if he touched her son, she'd kill him. She didn't care about herself, about watching her back, about staying out of jail. All that mattered now was her son and Megan.

Slinging her purse, she moved down the narrow hall to the door. The walls swayed a bit and she paused, waiting, then grabbed her jacket, threw open the door and walked out.

I hope pretty-boy Kel gets twenty to life as some guy's prison bitch.

Maurice was back in L.A. within two hours. Darcy, he thought, was still on the floor of that apartment.

He paced the spacious living room, staring at the boy tucked into his grandmother's side on the sofa. Delores Allen was just an added lure for Darcy. She was a drunk and liked all the things Maurice had given her to keep her quiet and docile. She didn't look docile now, though, glaring at him from her perch like a thin sparrow.

"Would you like a drink, Delores?" he asked. He knew she wanted one. She'd been drunk when he called her, drunk when she arrived by limousine. Twenty-four hours locked up made her look like an aging hooker in detox.

He stepped behind the maple-wood bar, pouring a scotch, then bringing it to her. She looked at it hungrily and Maurice knew she needed it—more than she wanted it.

"Go on, it will take the edge off."

She shook her head, hugging the sleeping child protectively. Maurice grinned and sipped the smooth, gold liquid. His gaze landed on the boy. He'd cried for his mother the instant he'd woken after the plane flight. He'd whimpered and whined, begging to go home. Maurice felt stung by it, wanting his boy to come to him. Maurice chose not to tell him he was his father and a little dose of his own insomnia medication had kept the boy quiet for now.

If he wasn't certain the child was his, he would have thought the boy belonged to another man. He was a dead ringer for Darcy. He even had her bright blue eyes. The only trait of his the child possessed was Maurice's dark hair, yet it was streaked with the same blond as his wife's.

Maurice turned away to stare out the window. The alarms were set, the fence electrified, and the dogs were loose on the grounds. There was no way she could get in here, yet Maurice wasn't taking any chances, keeping a gun close by. When she arrived, he'd call the police and claim she was trying to kidnap the child.

The boy stirred, whining for his mother, and Maurice motioned to a servant to give him the drug-laced milk. Maurice continued to look out the window, knowing Darcy couldn't get inside and confident he had the upper hand. He'd lure her in, then make her pay for ruining his life by leaving him. No one left him. And he wasn't going to let a pretty piece of poor, white trash win.

He'd kill her first.

Chapter 15

Darcy broke the speed limit and nearly crashed twice to get to Megan's place. She dashed out of the car, leaving it running and pushed through the front door, shouting for Charlie and Meg.

Only silence answered her.

She tore through the house, searching each room, noticing the overturned furniture, and that Charlie's backpack was gone.

"Meg!" she screamed, tears running down her face. "Meg!"

Her panic out of control, she raced out into the backyard and nearly fell over Meg sprawled facedown on the steps, the cordless phone inches from her hand. Darcy slid to her knees, checking her pulse.

"Oh, thank God." Bending, she pushed the curls back off her face. "Meg, wake up, honey, wake up." She tapped her face, rubbed her wrists.

Meg blinked and moaned.

Darcy felt as if the heavens opened up with hope. "Where are you hurt? Can you feel your legs and arms?"

Meg muttered, "Yes" and pushed up on her hands and knees.

"Where's Charlie, Meg?"

"He took him. Oh, Darcy," Meg cried, rolling onto her back. Darcy's eyes widened at the open cut on her cheek, and the blood smeared over her face and staining her clothes. It was dry. "He was so scared and I fought him, I swear, but he had a gun. He had a gun on Charlie!"

Darcy stared at Meg, helpless tears sliding down her cheeks. Then suddenly she hugged Meg, helping her upright.

"I swear I tried, he came out of nowhere. He ripped him right out of my arms! Charlie screamed and screamed and then…he stopped."

Darcy's heart stopped, too, then picked up speed. "I can't believe Kel did this!"

"No, Darcy. Maurice did."

Darcy froze. "He was here!"

"I grabbed the phone to dial the police, but he knocked me down. I went for his leg and that's when he backhanded me with the gun." Meg touched her face, wincing. "Jesus, I forgot how much that hurts."

"Come on, let's get you up."

Stuffing the phone in her back pocket, she helped Meg onto a lawn chair, then rushed inside for water and a cloth. Meg's cheek was cut, her left eye bruised. Maurice had had hit her so hard she wouldn't see out of that eye for days. Pistol-whipped. What a coward.

"Come inside."

Meg stood uneasily. "Darcy, I tried. You gotta believe me."

Darcy gripped her shoulders, meeting her gaze. "I don't doubt you, Meg. It's not your fault. It's mine."

She'd been too slow to take the signs for what they were, and should never have left Charlie alone. She'd walked right into a trap. She helped Meg into the house and into a chair, then hunted under the sink for a first-aid kit. Her hands shook as she cleaned Meg's wound and put a butterfly bandage on the cut. It was the best she could do right now. The blood was nearly dried and Darcy gave Meg an ice pack, then checked her watch. She'd been out cold for over eight hours.

She pulled out the phone and cleared the line. "You never got to the police?"

"No. I passed out."

Darcy handed her the phone. "Call them now."

"What? But you've been hiding all this time!"

"It ended when Maurice took my son. Where's your gun?"

Meg groaned. "Oh, Darcy, no."

Darcy's gaze pinned her. "Where is it, Meg?"

Letting out a sigh, Meg pointed to the soffit on the top cabinet. "The bullets are behind the flour, over the stove."

Darcy climbed on the counter, retrieved the weapon in the plastic bag, then found the ammo. "Call the cops."

"But…"

Darcy gave her a dark look and Meg nodded, sniffled, then just as she was about to dial, the phone rang in her hand. She answered it, frowning up at Darcy. Her eyes widened and she held it out.

"It's for you."

Darcy grabbed it. "Kel?"

"No, my love. It's your husband."

Darcy's stomach rolled loosely. He sounded so smooth and confident. "Where is my son?"

"You mean *our* son."

"No, he was never yours. You gave up that right when you tried to make me lose him. He's mine."

"Are you referring to the accident when you fell down the stairs? You always were clumsy, Darcy."

Darcy gritted her teeth, letting him talk, saving her

rage for when she met him face-to-face. She loaded bullets into the magazine.

"I want to talk with him."

"No."

"Let me talk to him, Maury!"

"He's sleeping peacefully."

They flew back to L.A., she realized. Good God, he had to have drugged Charlie to get him to go along without a fight.

"Charles will be all mine to raise when you go to jail for kidnapping him and keeping him from his loving father." He chuckled softly, a dignified sound, not too harsh, practiced. Darcy wanted to ram it down his throat. "You'll go to jail and never see him again."

With her palm, Darcy popped the magazine into the weapon and sighted down the barrel. "Don't count on it."

"What do you think you can do to me?"

"I'm going to let you experience that for yourself." She cut the line, laying down the phone, then stuffed the gun in the back of her slacks and pocketed the ammo.

"Darcy? What's happening?"

"Maurice has Charlie. He took Charlie for one reason. To lure me back to him." And have power over her, she thought. But then, Maurice had married a different woman.

"It's a trap and you know it." Meg held out the cordless phone. "You have to wait for the police now, Darcy. It's kidnapping. Let the FBI handle this."

"No, this is my problem, my son and my husband." Darcy headed to the door. *Time for some payback.*

Meg called out to her. "What do I tell the police?"

"Everything." Darcy was out the door and in her car within seconds. Police sirens roared in the distance as she sped in the other direction. She needed to get to L.A. as fast as she could and wanted to fly, but Maurice would likely have his hired creeps waiting for her. It would take her a few hours by car. She needed the upper hand.

But first, she needed some equipment.

And the help of the Cassandras.

Darcy was scrapping for a fight, feeling like a junkyard dog, mean and willing to bite hard on anyone who got in her way. She'd packed her equipment, clothes and some things for Charlie and pushed the legal side of the speed limit. There was no use charging in without a plan. It would only give Maurice a bigger advantage and that wouldn't do her son any good.

She was going to get Charlie back the safest way possible.

Rage and worry simmered as she drove the six

hours to Los Angeles. Maurice would be waiting for her in Bel Air. If he wanted to come out of this smelling like a rose, then he wouldn't lay a hand on her son. It was the only thing keeping her from busting into the estate and shooting him on the spot. She rented a hotel room, tried to sleep and couldn't. She was prepared, waiting for the timing to be right.

Darcy slowed her walk through the west end of Bel Air, high heels clicking on the concrete. Her leather slacks made her thighs rub and sounded like a squeegee on a clean window. It was annoying, but the dark cream leather outfit gave her the look of money and sophistication. Natural and unnoticed in Bel Air. It helped that her wig was black and her face bore the bone structure of an actress whom she knew lived this time of year in Tahoe.

She walked past Maurice's estate. Just looking at it brought back the memories of Maurice pushing her down the stairs and smiling while he did it, of him locking her up in the guest room for days without food, when he'd used sex as a weapon, tying her to the bed. Though he hadn't been violent then, it had been against her will.

Old fear made her body perspire under her clothes and she shook the memories loose, focusing on her plan. It was still a couple hours till dusk.

Surrounding the house and land was a two-foot-thick stone wall with a gate that was twice the size

of a Mack truck. It was electrified and on automatic
from a keypad inside and a handheld sensor for entering from the street. Maurice hadn't left the house.
And no one had come in.

The west end of the property faced the water, the
view open to the sea. Darcy could have swum to it
and walked up onto the beach if not for the laser
alarms near the water's edge. Maurice had a boat in
a slip a few blocks up the coast, but he never set foot
in the ocean. He couldn't swim well.

A car moved up beside her, slowing. She heard the
window electronically go down. Great, a pick-up line.

Then a deep voice said, "Get in, now."

She stilled and turned her head. Jack. He leaned
and pushed open the passenger door.

Darcy let out a breath and climbed in. "How did
you know?" She was wearing a mask.

"After two years, you ask that?" Jack pulled away
and drove out of the area. "Are you nuts?"

"He has Charlie."

"I know, Megan called me. The police are with
her. Let them handle it, dammit."

"I can't. He's got my son!" Darcy rubbed her
forehead, a thousand thoughts tripping through her
head and slamming against a wall. "What the hell am
I supposed to do? The man tried to kill me and he
has Charlie. Do you understand? He has my baby!"

"He wants *you*."

"I don't give a shit what Maurice wants! My child is in danger! Don't interfere, I can handle this."

"Baby," he said softly, and immediately tears sprang into her eyes and her lips quivered. Jesus, this man could get to her so easily. "I know you can. I'm on your side."

She pulled off the wig and fluffed her hair then carefully peeled the mask off as she spoke. "I'm glad you are, Jack, really. But I have to do this alone. This man has made my life hell for years and I just found the guts to fight him at his own game."

"He won't hurt Charlie, he wants you and you're walking into a trap."

"I don't have a choice."

"Yes, you do. The FBI has all the evidence on Fairchild and Maurice."

"What?" She looked at him, horrified.

"I gave it to them. Don't look at me like that, woman. It's the only way, and you know it. You have to let the authorities in or nothing will stand up in court. After seeing your evidence, Agent Bale has agreed to open a case on Fairchild. They'll have to review it before they go to Maurice."

"That isn't going to make a difference."

"It will when we find the body."

She shook her head. "Maurice covers his tracks really well, Jack. He was careful when he beat me where anyone could see the damage."

"I still find it hard to believe you stood for that."

"I didn't. He lost a couple teeth to prove it. But he didn't have to hit me to be abusive. Good God, when I was pregnant with Charlie, he threatened to cut him out of me."

"Jesus, what a son of a bitch. I'm not going to ask why you married a man like that."

"I grew up poor with an alcoholic mother, and he was rich, famous and wanted *me*. I just didn't realize the price would be my self-esteem and pride."

Jack reached for her, urging her closer. "That's been over for a long time."

Darcy sighed against him, her head on his shoulder. "We need to find the body."

"The warehouse?" he said.

"I thought of that. But I was in there, and didn't find one. You know a decomposing body would smell."

He reached in his jacket and pulled out a slip of paper, reading it and driving. "Do you know what ah…HCHO is? It's urea-formaldehyde."

She straightened in the seat. "It's an adhesive used on fiber, wood movie sets and 3-D background paintings to preserve color and seal the surface. Set designers need it to maintain the integrity of background paintings while filming for months at a time."

"Well, that's what's on the burned clothes." He

handed her the report. "And they were mono-grammed, Darcy, with his full name."

Her mind started clicking. "Take a left here."

He did.

"You wouldn't happen to have your old badge, would you?" He gestured to the glove box. She found it, and for a second ran her fingers over the gold shield. "Detective, huh? Would your sister like that you quit because of her?"

"No, she wouldn't. You'd have liked her." The sadness in his tone punched a hole in her heart.

"I know I would have." She kissed his cheek.

"So what's up your sleeve?"

"Use this to get in the gate." She handed him the shield. "I'll tell you where to go."

Jack's badge did the trick, and Darcy directed him to the Studio Eight warehouse. It was late afternoon, and shooting was done for the day except for night filming on other lots. The area was deserted. She climbed out and went to the warehouse door.

She cursed. "My lock picks are in my hotel."

Jack nudged her out of the way and with his own, opened the lock. She looked at him. "I'm impressed."

"Bounty hunting gives you certain advantages a cop doesn't have."

They opened the door, the seal popping loudly. Jack flicked on the light.

"You don't care if we're seen?"

"I'm calling the police as soon as we're sure."

"You sound awfully confident."

"You've been right all along so far." He winked at her, then gestured to the cylinders and barrels, the rolls of cord and cases. "You know what all this stuff is for?"

"Yeah. Some of it's corrosive—acids, ammonia. But the HCHO is over there." She pointed to the back. They moved together.

"God that stinks," he said.

"I know. When I was in here before it made me sick, light-headed. I almost got caught. I wrote down all the chemicals stored in here, but with all that's been going on, I didn't have a chance to research all of them. HCHO was one of the chemicals listed, but I didn't realize it was formaldehyde."

She inspected the barrels, finding nothing untoward. "So what do we do, open them all?"

"Where is the one that leaked?"

She tried to remember where she'd stood, moving from her hiding spot then pretending to go back into the warehouse as she had for her bag. "Here, this one."

Jack knelt, touching his fingers to the concrete floor then bringing them to his nose. "This is it." He looked around. "We need a crowbar."

"The chemicals aren't opened in here, Jack, they're taken to the sets. There won't be one."

He went to his car, coming back with the tire iron. He pried up the lid.

Darcy's heart pounded, half of her hoping, and the other wishing that Porche Fairchild hadn't paid with her life. The lid popped and Jack used the tire iron to swirl the liquid.

Nothing.

"Damn."

He looked at the bases of the barrels. "We have to open them all."

She crossed to a row of three and stilled, something catching her eye. She moved to the back where the cylinders were lined up like soldiers. She tried moving one.

"Help me move this."

He came to her, straining to move the cylinder. "Why am I doing this?" he said.

"Look, can you see in there, between the cylinders? There's something back there and it's shorter." She pointed upward to the tops of the cylinders. "And there's a gap."

"They aren't lined up against the wall."

"Yeah, but there's so many, who'd notice?"

Jack moved another; it took a few minutes. They weighed in excess of a hundred pounds.

In the center of the CO_2 cylinders, there was a barrel. Jack looked at her, then got the tire iron to pry up the lid. It didn't pop like the others.

Darcy realized instantly that Maurice hadn't done his research. Most of the chemicals in here were corrosive, or explosive. Except HCHO. He thought it would disintegrate the body, instead, it preserved it. The night she'd lured him here, he'd checked to be certain the container was still hidden, but had no way he could remove it. So here it had remained. If he'd known the components and put her in another barrel, she'd have had nothing to prove him a killer.

Darcy didn't have to look close.

Jack didn't have to stir the chemical.

Porche Fairchild was there.

Perfectly preserved.

So much so that even her hairstyle was still in place.

Jack lifted his gaze. "Now, we call the police."

Darcy smiled. "I hope you have friends, because we could be charged with breaking and entering."

It only took the police a few minutes to get there and suddenly it was chaos. Police, forensics, studio officials and chemical experts crowded the area. The barrel was removed with Porche still inside and taken to the crime lab. Darcy had answered several questions and met Agent Bale. She freely offered her DNA, her shoes and prints, but by the time that was done, the place was lit up like a premiere and there were people everywhere, working, or there to gawk.

Jack, she noticed, was in detective mode, and Darcy backed away from the crowd, heading toward the gate. Jack was going to be mad, but she had to leave. Now. Maurice would be nailed to the wall in a couple of days.

But Charlie was still in danger now.

She couldn't waste another moment.

Chapter 16

Without a moon, there were no shadows.

Beyond the occasional streetlight or headlights, it was a soot-black night. Perfect. Crouched in the dark on a property across the wide street, Darcy watched the estate. A couple of the staff departed, leaving one car in the driveway. Maurice's BMW would be in the garage under a tarp.

She didn't have much time. When Jack realized she was missing, the cavalry would come and there was no telling what Maurice would do. She had to get Charlie out first.

Darcy removed a small package from her pack before slipping it on her back. The cat suit was black, and she wore a vest over it, zipped to her throat, more for storing a few things than for warmth. She tucked the small package in a vest pocket, then rose to a crouch, ran across the street and ducked into the shadows.

She approached from the east, on a neighboring property, beyond the blind spot of the security cameras she remembered from when she'd left Maurice. She shined a penlight at the camera, counting off the seconds it took for it to pan the yard and return. From her pack, she pulled out a thermal blanket with a thick rubber backing. Getting past the electrified wires on the top of the stone wall wouldn't be easy. But she was more worried about the dogs. They weren't pets, they were attack dogs. If she wasn't quick, she'd be ripped apart before she could get to Charlie.

She climbed the large tree beside the fence on the neighbor's property. They didn't have Maurice's security paranoia, but she still had to avoid the sensors. She wished she could risk the strength of the tree limb and just move out to the edge, but if it cracked, they'd hear it for half a block. Like a lizard, she lay facedown on the branch, then scooted inch by inch out onto the limb, balancing herself with her ankles wrapped around the thick branch.

In one quick motion, she unrolled the blanket, throwing it toward the wall and letting it sail open to drape over electrical wires as thin as hair. Gripping the branch, she rolled off, dangling for a second before swinging her legs up and throwing her weight at the wall. She caught the edge, praying the blanket didn't slip out from under her as she flung her leg over. Sitting on the ledge, she watched the cameras pan, then jumped.

Immediately she heard the dogs growling, the soft thump of their paws as they raced toward her. Quickly Darcy pulled the package from her vest, but in seconds she was cornered, the black Dobermans baring their teeth and barking.

She unwrapped the raw meat and stretched out her arm. One dog snapped at her.

"Easy, Hercules," she whispered and the dog cocked its head. "Hello, Zeus, how's it going, buddy?" Her voice was hushed, the meat hanging from her fingers. The growling was a low constant hum. Before she left Maurice she'd secretly fed the dogs so they'd obey her and wouldn't bark when Rainy came to help her escape. She tossed the meat to the left near the wall, but the dogs didn't go for it.

Now what?

Tugging off her glove, she extended her arm. The dogs growled, shiny fangs bright in the dark. Darcy didn't think she'd ever been more afraid of being eaten. She let them sniff her.

One whimpered. One sat.

"Go on, eat." They just stared, their growls low and steady. Then she remembered the commands, and motioned sharply to the meat and said, "Eat."

The deadly black pair went for the food. Quickly, Darcy backed against the wall, blending into the dark, glancing down at the dogs. The drugged meat would put them out cold for at least a couple hours. Harmless drugs, but necessary. Pulling on her gloves, she moved swiftly along the perimeter toward the back patio where she was able to see a considerable part of the lower level through the great room. With the lights on inside, no one could see her.

She edged around the house, remembering when she'd selected the flowers and bushes, the curtains and furniture. Maurice had given her free rein and endless money to decorate. It had been a blanket covering the truth about her husband. There was always a price with Maurice. That was how he'd gotten Kel Adams to do what he wanted.

She slipped over the low retaining wall that cupped the back patio, her felt-and-rubber-bottomed shoes soundless. She heard music, Bach, and knew Maurice was near. She inched along the outer wall of the house, sliding up to each window and looking in. The floor plan in the house was etched in her mind, the way in, the way out. Darcy knew she had to find Charlie first.

The great room was empty, the low light spilling

softly over the decor. It looked just as it had when she left. Nothing had been changed. Even her wedding picture still hung over the mantel.

A shadow flickered, and Darcy's gaze shot to the walls, then to her surroundings. It moved again and her gaze zeroed in on the lower guest-bathroom window to her left. Darcy rushed to it, peering.

Oh, crap. Her mother!

What the hell was she doing here? First instinct was that her mother was in on this. She still hadn't forgiven Delores for not helping her when she needed her mother's understanding the most. But Darcy wasn't leaving her mom behind. And if she was drunk? Getting to Charlie was one thing—getting her mother out as well was another.

Darcy watched Delores fill a glass of water and leave the bathroom. Quickly she moved to the next window. Her heart skipped a beat when she saw Charlie on the bed, motionless. Delores held his head, tipping the glass to his lips.

Charlie was pale as a sheet and not moving. *Damn you, Maurice!*

She squatted to rethink the plan. If Charlie was drugged, then he'd be tough to carry out of the house with any speed. And her mother—drunk? Or not?

The dull rumble of voices pierced the quiet, and she hurried along the length of the house. There was a long breezeway leading from the house to the garage with doors to the side lot where the servants parked.

Strapping on her NVGs Darcy shifted around the bushes and leaped the north patio wall to see who was leaving for the night. Two women hurried down the glass corridor, one glancing back at the house. When the first woman stopped, the other grabbed her, shaking her head.

They knew and did nothing.

Darcy moved along the west side of the breezeway, then around the garage to the east side. One woman punched in the lock code. Darcy inched closer. She ought to knock one out and take a uniform, but the maids usually lived in the house. Which meant Maurice had sent them home for a reason.

One woman stepped out, then the second. Darcy slipped up behind them and caught the door, darting past. It closed without her being noticed. The lock clicked shut, the alarm light turning from green to red.

Inside the breezeway, she stored the NVGs in the pack then moved down the hall toward the main house. Outside the kitchen door, Darcy concealed a couple of her knives. The gun was a last resort, in a holster under her left arm and hidden by the vest.

She opened the door slowly, her gaze shooting around the kitchen. To the left was the dining room, to the right and beyond the separating wall was the foyer and stairs leading to the second floor. She hoped her mother and Charlie stayed on the lower level. If they didn't, she'd have a tough time getting upstairs then back down.

Part of her needed to confront Maurice, but her maternal instincts wanted her son out as safely and silently as possible.

She stepped inside.

She moved through the kitchen, alert to sounds. She needed to locate Maurice first and suspected he'd be in his office to the left of the foyer, next to the library. Music still played, muffling any sound she'd make. She followed it, then realized it was over the in-house speaker system. Where was he then?

She moved through the house, to the foyer where she'd landed when he'd pushed her down the stairs, then beyond. The door to the library was open, but the room was empty. The door to his office was closed. Keeping back so she didn't cast a shadow on the floor in front of the door, Darcy listened. She was nearly certain Maurice wasn't in there till a chair squeaked. She darted back, flat against the wall. His high-backed oxblood leather chair, which looked like a throne, had always made that sound. Retracing her steps, she passed through the kitchen, crossed the dining room and into the back hall.

Her mother was talking to Charlie, but her son

wasn't responding. Darcy checked the unopened doors before slipping into the guest room.

She reached her mother just as Charlie opened his eyes. "Mom!"

Her mother turned, and Darcy covered their mouths, hushing them with a warning look.

Her mother just stared at her, her gaze moving over the cat suit, the knives. "I didn't have anything to do with this."

Darcy glared at her mother to be quiet as she scooped up her child, hugging him tightly. She checked him for injuries, noticing his pupils were dilated, then motioned for him to stay quiet. Darcy pulled out her cell, hitting send, and she let the call ring once, then cut the line. Her own cavalry would come now. She took a step. Her mother stood there, immobile. Darcy inclined her head for Delores to follow.

Down the hall and into the dining room, Darcy made a decision to take the shortest distance and headed toward the great room. If she could get out without Maurice knowing, she'd consider it a miracle. But she couldn't shut off the alarms. Maurice was paranoid about security and changed the codes all the time. Even if she tried the breezeway doors, the floodlights would come on, and every window and door would lock down. It was how he kept her trapped in here.

They edged the room, behind the sofas and tables to the French doors leading to the back patio deck. Darcy set Charlie down to cut the sensor wires in the glass door.

"Well, aren't you the clever girl."

Darcy whipped around.

Maurice was standing on the far side of the great room near the Roman columns, a cocktail in his hand. He smiled and a chill rippled all the way down her spine.

"Hello, my love." He looked her over thoroughly, walking closer. "You've lost weight, haven't you?"

Her lips thinned. She put herself between Maurice and her family.

"You were stupid to even try this, you know that, don't you?"

He spoke to her the way he had four years ago, reasonable, as if making him mad over something trivial was her fault, as if the threats to her life were her doing. It just pissed her off more.

"Bite me, Maurice."

"Interesting proposition, but my tastes have changed."

"You have taste?"

His expression sharpened and he tsked. "Sarcasm doesn't become you, Darcy." He set the glass down and shrugged his jacket into place. It set off a warning in Darcy. He always did that before he hit her, before he pushed her down the stairs.

Maurice moved closer, eyeing her. "I like the longer blond hair better. That reddish mess doesn't suit you."

She said nothing.

"And what do you think you are, dressed like that?"

He moved closer and she advanced, not about to let him near the only exit and her child.

The dignified act slid away and he lunged for her. Darcy tipped her body, her foot shooting out and hitting Maurice in the chest. He flew backward, banging into a delicate table, sending the lamp and knickknacks across the floor.

Maurice gasped for air, clutching the table ledge, glaring at her. "You deserve a beating for that, *bitch*."

He came at her and Darcy struck first, one to the face, a second to his stomach. But Maurice was fit and took the brunt of it easily, locking his arm around her throat. She went loose, sliding down and twisting. He tightened his grip, held her back against him.

"Fighting me just makes it all the more interesting," he growled in her ear. "Now what, my *love?*" He jerked tighter, cutting off her air.

She answered in successive moves. She threw her head back into his nose, drove her elbow into his stomach, then snapped her fist down to slam into his groin.

He grunted each time, howling with the last. She

shoved him away, turned, fist primed. He was folding to the floor.

Charlie moved.

"No!" she shouted.

Maurice surged and grabbed Charlie's leg. Darcy went after him till he pulled a tazer from his pocket. He held it crackling near her son's skin.

Darcy froze. "Don't, Maurice."

"Give up then."

She said nothing, trying to ignore the fear in her son's eyes.

Maurice gave the tazer a jolt, blue current sparking. "This is supposed to take down a two-hundred-pound man, what will it do to a child?"

It would kill him. Maurice knew it.

She threw her hands up. "Okay, okay, don't hurt him."

Maurice climbed to his feet, using Charlie as a shield as he moved toward her. Charlie whimpered.

"Shut up." He shook her son violently.

"You do that again, Maury, and I swear to God I'll scar you for life."

Maurice let the tazer crackle, the blue stream of energy too close to her child's throat. Then he backhanded her, snapping her head to the side. Slowly, she turned her head, leveling him with a stare meant to fry the flesh from his bones. She swiped her hand across her lip. Blood smeared.

Maurice's confidence slipped a little.

Between them, Charlie sobbed, staring up at her with his big eyes and trusting her to free him. Moving back, Darcy circled, making Maurice turn, making him look at her and not her son.

"This is between me and you, Maury. Let him go."

He didn't, holding Charlie by the collar of his shirt. "You'll be my wife again."

"Dream on." She moved to the right.

"Or you'll go to jail for kidnapping."

"I protected myself and my son." She wanted to draw him near the fallen knickknacks, make him trip. She needed Charlie clear of him. "You're the one going to jail, Maury."

"For what?" he said supremely arrogant.

"Forgery, illegal money transfer, defrauding the government and there is the matter of Porche Fairchild."

His face turned to stone. "I heard she's still on sabbatical."

"She's dead."

"Really. You kill her?"

"No, you did. Lot eight, the studio? Ring a bell? I found her body in a barrel of HCHO."

He paled, but covered it well. "That doesn't mean anything to me."

"It should. Remember when you burned the bloody clothes in the hearth? You passed out, and I put out the flames and took them. They have her blood and the HCHO all over them. Plus your monogram—and your DNA."

Slowly the color drained from his handsome face.

"And I'll give you one guess who has them now."

"Well, it seems you've grown a brain." He lunged, the tazer out, and Darcy swung her leg up, clipping his wrist. The tazer flew out of his hand and he stumbled right on her, dragging Charlie. She brought both fists down on the back of his neck.

He dropped like a stone, taking Charlie with him. Darcy pulled her son away, pushing him toward her mother. Delores grabbed the tazer and stood near the door with Charlie behind her and the weapon out. Her hand shook.

"Now you have no way out." Maurice pushed up on his hands.

"You are so stupid sometimes." Darcy moved backward toward the French doors. "Do you think I came here alone?"

Maurice's expression turned molten, the ramifications sliding through his brain. "I'll kill you!" He got to his feet, swaying a little.

"You tried that once." Fists out, she flicked her fingers. "I'll give you another chance, though. Close your eyes, Charlie, Mommy has some house cleaning to do."

Maurice charged at her and Darcy waited for one

moment. Waited till he was nearly on her. Her fists shot out in rapid succession, breaking his nose. Blood poured and he stumbled back, swiping at his face and staring at the blood. Then he came at her, and she drove her fist into his solar plexus. He buckled over, gasping, then threw his head back, clipping her under her chin. Darcy tripped backward, putting distance between them.

"You can't testify against me, Darcy," he snarled. "A wife can't testify against her husband!"

"You really need to come out of the movie world, Maury. A wife can't be *forced* to testify. Nobody will twist my arm."

"You spent the money, bitch!" he roared advancing. "You decorated this house with it."

"I never signed a thing. Remember? You wouldn't let me."

The instant he was near, she executed a high spin kick, knocking him in the side of the head. He fell against the grand column, grabbing it for support. Darcy wasn't done. Another double kick packed with anger sent him flying back. He landed hard on the tile floor, sliding a few feet.

He didn't move.

Darcy adjusted her stance, not trusting that he was out for the count.

"My God in heaven Darcy, where did you learn that?"

"Athena Academy." Darcy rushed to the doors. Taking the tazer, she shocked the alarm system on the door. It shorted out and the locks sprang. She scooped up Charlie and shoved her mother out ahead of herself.

Maurice was still on his back.

Outside, she heard the blare of sirens, the squeal of tires. But it was the sweet sound of the incoming chopper that alerted half the neighborhood. Lights blinked on for a block as Darcy raced out, helping her mother run toward the beach.

Like a hawk diving for its prey, the helicopter swooped in from the shoreline. The blades beat the air, the power knocking over planters, bending back tree limbs. The pilot delicately lowered the iron bird, and Darcy smiled at Lieutenant Josie Lockworth as she touched down.

God, it was good to have heavy-duty backup.

Darcy hurried her family toward the chopper.

Maurice screamed her name. "If I lose it all, so do you!"

Midstride, Darcy turned her head to look behind. Maurice stood on the patio and pointed a gun at her back. He cocked the hammer. She stopped and put Charlie down, telling him to run to the chopper, pushing her mother with him. Josie was already leaning out to pull them in.

"Darcy! Come on!" Josie shouted when Charlie and Delores were inside.

Darcy met her gaze and put her hands up in surrender, then made small circular motions with one gloved finger. Josie's gaze shifted beyond to Maurice and her lips tightened. She didn't want to leave her, Darcy knew. Darcy shook her head and mouthed, *Save my baby.* Josie adjusted her headset and lifted off without her.

"Don't shoot, Maurice." Behind her, he smiled and Darcy looked up as the chopper rose, putting her hands behind her head.

Charlie was screaming for her, reaching, and her mother struggled to hold on to him.

The helicopter blades twisted the air, stirring dirt and leaves, the water in the pool. Josie aimed the spotlight down like a beam from heaven, showering them in white light.

Maurice fired a shot at the chopper and in one motion Darcy twisted, pulling a knife from the pocket behind her neck. She threw. The small blade whistled through the air and sank into his thigh.

He howled, tottering backward, grabbing the hilt and yanking it out. For a split second, he stared at the blade. "You really think that made a difference!" He threw it aside and extended his arm, aiming.

But Darcy was already sighting down a .9mm barrel.

Maurice's eyes widened.

"You fired a gun at my son, my mother and my

friend," she said with each step closer. "You pathetic little *worm.*"

His gaze flicked to the chopper lifting higher, the TV news van crew spilling from the van, already filming. But Darcy's attention was on his face, his finger on the trigger.

"ABS cameras are rolling. It's over Maurice. You're on national news trying to kill your wife and son. You're ruined."

His face twisted with rage and he pulled the trigger. Darcy lunged right and heard the shot whiz by her as she returned fire. Her bullet impacted his shoulder, knocking him to the ground. Rushing forward, she kicked the gun out of his hand.

He clutched his shoulder, breathing hard. Blood fountained between his fingers. "I'll make you pay for this. This is assault! I won't go to jail, you know it. I *own* people!"

"All that money, and you're still such a loser." She pointed the gun at his head, breathing hard. "Payback's a real bitch, ain't it?"

For the first time, she saw real fear in his eyes.

"Darcy?"

The familiar voice floated to her, clear and determined. *Jack.*

"Don't. He's not worth it."

At the sound of Jack's voice, Darcy felt something invigorating slide through her and she lowered the pistol. Maurice deflated like a spent balloon.

"You're not going to die, Maurice. That's too easy. You're going to live in the same hell you put me in."

Suddenly cops were everywhere, one man checking Maurice for weapons, then pulling him off the ground. He groaned, bleeding all over himself. He could barely stand.

An officer clamped on handcuffs, ignoring Maurice's wince of pain.

Darcy moved close, in his face. "You know what, Maury?" she said, disgusted. "I want a divorce."

Chapter 17

Darcy turned away from Maurice and let the cops search her, but her gaze was on Jack standing a few feet away.

Her eyes teared, the tension of the past hours flowing out of her in hard breaths. Her son and mother were safe in the air with Josie. Maurice was in handcuffs.

And Jack was here.

When the police had her knives and Meg's gun, she lowered her arms. For a second, she just stared at Jack. Then he rushed to her, clamping his arms around her. He buried his face in the side of her neck.

"Woman, are you ever going to stop scaring me like this?"

Darcy closed her eyes, tears of relief falling. "Yes, I promise. No more," she said and he leaned back to look her in the eyes.

"What made you think you could—"

She pressed two fingers to his lips. "I had a plan, you know." She gestured to the news van, the chopper that was circling the estate.

"Athena graduates?"

"Yeah, they're the best kind of people." She glanced back toward the parking area. "Go, Tory."

Tory Patton kept the cameras on Maurice, shoving her microphone in his face, asking him why he had tried to kill his wife. Maurice just glared at Darcy as she walked with Jack toward the gathering of flashing lights and cameras.

The police read Maurice his rights, and Darcy watched as they put him in a cruiser.

"Did they find Kel or whatever his name is?"

Jack gestured to a police cruiser. "The actor didn't go far from Hollywood." Darcy marched up to the car. Jack grabbed her back.

"I want to punch his lights out."

"I took care of that for you."

Darcy blinked, then looked at Kel. He had a black eye and a split lip.

Smiling, Darcy grabbed Jack's right hand and kissed the scrape. "You're such a knight," she said.

"I figured if you got a hold of him, he wouldn't be fit for trial."

She smiled.

The chopper hovered, then like a feather falling gracefully to the ground, Josie set it down on the front lawn. The blades beat slower as the door slid back and her mother hopped out, hair whipping as she reached for Charlie.

Darcy ducked and ran near, grabbing up her son. She met Josie's gaze through the windshield. "Thank you," Darcy said, though she knew Josie couldn't hear above the noise.

Grinning, Josie threw her a salute. Darcy hurried her mother away from the chopper and Josie lifted off, swooping high and out of sight.

"Men are in real danger if Athena produces women with guts like you three," Jack said, walking up behind her.

Charlie shrieked Jack's name and lunged into his arms. Jack held her son tightly, then wrapped his arm around her and pressed his lips to her temple. "No more secrets, Darcy, no more."

"A girl has to have a few. How else can I keep a man interested?"

Jack smiled. "It wasn't your secrets that kept me around, darlin'." He pressed his forehead to hers, both releasing a heavy sigh. Then he kissed her, staking his claim. And Darcy let him.

Oh, glory glory, she thought happily. *Let freedom ring.*

Several months later

Darcy stared at her mother. Her drinking had aged her. She was only about fifty but looked sixty-five.

It had been six months since Maurice's arrest. The trial had been the sensation of Hollywood. Televised and drawn out. She'd testified, staring Maurice down in the courtroom. Her mother had confirmed the details, and Darcy had watched her humiliate herself on the witness stand to do it.

Darcy had seen Delores only once since then. Now she was asking to be a part of their lives.

"I'm sorry, Darcy. If I hadn't been drinking maybe I could have gotten Charlie out or helped you."

"Yes, you're right, but Maurice wasn't giving up easily." Her mother seemed to crumble a little.

Darcy studied her, remembering her childhood, all the things her mother had done for her to try to make her life better. She'd worked two jobs, made her clothes, and it wasn't until she'd remarried for the third time that the drinking had started. One day they'd have to sit down and understand why she sank into a bottle. They were all frail, she thought, each with fears and lost hopes. And Darcy had a feeling her mother hadn't experienced a lot of love in the past years.

She reached out, gazing into her mother's eyes, and said the words her mother needed to hear. "I forgive you, Mom. We all make mistakes. Sometimes we pay for them for a long time."

Delores's eyes teared and she whispered, "Thank you."

Darcy hesitated for a second. "I want you to know that I really can't let you near Charlie till you're sober and willing to go for treatment."

"I know, I know. I have been to AA meetings." When Darcy's look doubted, she showed her the chips awarded for sober months.

Darcy smiled, genuinely pleased. "I have to be able to trust you."

"Honey, I know. I have to trust me, too." She looked longingly out into the backyard where Charlie was playing with his new puppy. "Some things are worth it."

Darcy held back her tears and said, "Go on, Mom."

Delores met her gaze, her eyes glossy. She sniffled and gripped her daughter's hand. "Thank you, Darcy. I'm so proud of you, you know. So very proud."

Darcy kissed her cheek, and then because she needed it more, she hugged her mother, whispering that she was proud of her, too.

When they parted, Delores's gaze shifted past her daughter. Darcy turned.

Jack sipped coffee, his shoulder braced on the doorjamb. Like an excited child, Delores went outside to Charlie.

"I know what it took to forgive her," he said.

"Not as much as I thought." Darcy watched her mother kick off her shoes and drop to the ground with Charlie. There was a comfortable silence between them before she asked, "So, are you going back on the force?"

"What do you want?"

She met his gaze. "I have what I want. My son, my real name back, my divorce. My shop's doing well without me there 24/7 so I get more time with Charlie."

Jack's smile was patient. "You're missing the point."

"Jack, it's not my life, not my decision. But I'd rather you be a detective than on the street chasing crazies."

"Why?"

"Because I don't want you to get hurt."

"Why?"

She made a frustrated sound, fidgeting. "Because I really like you."

"Like?" He looked insulted.

"Jeez, Jack, what do you want from me?"

He pushed off the wall and set his cup down, then

slid his arms around her. He pulled her against him, every inch of them sealed together.

"I want the truth. The honest to God truth. There's no one to hide from, no one after you. You still have your network, though most of it's illegal as hell."

"Jack," she warned. "I'm trying to make it all legal, you know that."

"Yeah, yeah."

She smoothed her hand up his arms to his big shoulders. "So what's this big truth you want to know?"

He brushed her hair off her face. "Tell me… what's in your heart, Darcy?"

She gazed up at him, feeling as if they were standing on the edge of a cliff and not in her kitchen.

"You, Jack."

His smile was warm and slow. "Yeah?"

"Oh, yeah. Deep in there." She plowed her fingers into his hair, tipping his head near. "You're sorta like that stray dog that won't go away." He snickered. "I'll keep you around."

"And around and around and around," he murmured against her mouth, then kissed her with all the hunger she'd been longing for in a lifetime.

Soon she'd tell him how much she loved him. How she wanted to share her new life with him. But it was new to her, this freedom. She was trying it on still, still learning about the woman she was meant to be.

Jack seemed to know her already. He'd seen beneath the masks, understood who was hidden behind the alias. And he'd stayed beside her, with quiet strength, as she rediscovered her freedom.

He'd wait for her, till it fit right.

Because if Darcy knew anything about Jack, it was that he had infinite reserves of patience.

And she hoped, persistence.

* * * * *

Books by Amy J. Fetzer

Silhouette Bombshell

Alias #6

Harlequin Intrigue

Under His Protection #733

ATHENA FORCE

Chosen for their talents.
Trained to be the best.

Expected to change the world.

The women of Athena Academy
share an unforgettable experience
and an unbreakable bond—until
one of their own is murdered.

The adventure begins with these six books:

PROOF by Justine Davis, July 2004

ALIAS by Amy J. Fetzer, August 2004

EXPOSED by Katherine Garbera,
September 2004

DOUBLE-CROSS by Meredith Fletcher,
October 2004

PURSUED by Catherine Mann, November 2004

JUSTICE by Debra Webb, December 2004

**And look for six more Athena Force stories
January to June 2005.**

Available at your favorite retail outlet.

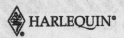

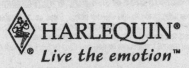

If you enjoyed what you just read,
then we've got an offer you can't resist!

Take 2 bestselling love stories FREE!
Plus get a FREE surprise gift!

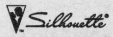

SPECIAL EDITION™

A Texas Tale

by

JUDITH LYONS
(Silhouette Special Edition #1637)

Crissy Albreit was a bona fide risk taker
as part of the daredevil troupe the
Alpine Angels. But Tate McCade was
offering a risk even Crissy wasn't sure
she wanted to take: move to Texas and
run the ranch her good-for-nothing
father left behind after his death. Crissy
long ago said goodbye to her past.
Now this McCade guy came bearing
a key to it? And maybe even one to
her future as well....

*Available September 2004
at your favorite retail outlet.*